PRAISE FOR LEE HARRIS AND HER CHRISTINE BENNETT MYSTERIES

"An excellent series."
—*Pittsburgh Tribune-Review*

"A not-to-miss series."
—*Mystery Scene*

"Harris's holiday series . . . a strong example of the suburban cozy."
—*Ellery Queen's Mystery Magazine*

"Extremely popular . . . Chris is a wonderful heroine."
—*Romantic Times Magazine*

"Inventive plotting and sharp, telling characterization make the Lee Harris novels a pure pleasure to read."
—ROBERT BARNARD

By Lee Harris

Published by Fawcett Books:

THE HAPPY BIRTHDAY MURDER

Lee Harris

FAWCETT BOOKS • NEW YORK
The Ballantine Publishing Group

A Fawcett Book
Published by The Ballantine Publishing Group
Copyright © 2002 by Lee Harris

All rights reserved under International and Pan-American Copyright Conventions. Published in the United States by The Ballantine Publishing Group, a division of Random House, Inc., New York, and simultaneously in Canada by Random House of Canada Limited, Toronto.

Fawcett and colophon are trademarks of Random House, Inc.

www.ballantinebooks.com

ISBN 0-449-00702-2

Manufactured in the United States of America

First Edition: February 2002

OPM 10 9 8 7 6 5 4 3 2

For my son, Josh,
who loves the cake, if not the birthday.

The author thanks, as always,
Ana M. Soler
and James L. V. Wegman,
without whom there would be no series.

And, after all, what is a lie? 'Tis but
The truth in masquerade; and I defy
Historians, heroes, lawyers, priests, to put
A fact without some leaven of a lie.

—LORD BYRON
    Don Juan, Canto XI, Stanza 37
    1823

PROLOGUE

Even when I was single and lived in this house alone, I felt secure in it. It's one of the older houses on our street, a street that was partially built up in the Fifties and Sixties and then completed, by a different builder in a totally different style, ten to fifteen years later. The ground-floor exterior is brick, the upstairs wood, and the roof was replaced not long before I was released from my vows at St. Stephen's and took up residence here. The house had been my aunt's for as long as I can remember, and she took good care of it.

When Jack, my policeman-turned-lawyer husband, joined me in the house after our marriage, he put his own skills to use making it even more secure. He updated the locks on the doors and windows, replaced a couple of windowpanes that had mysteriously cracked, and had a mason come over and look at the brickwork. I put my foot down on an alarm system, choosing to believe that I could trust my neighbors to spot unwanted strangers in the area, which isn't hard to do when almost no one parks on the street and passersby tend to be children going to or coming from school or their parents.

Once, a long time ago, Aunt Margaret did combat with a mouse in the kitchen. Aunt Margaret won and generations of mice have been frightened away since then, for which I am grateful. And the basement, where the furnace and hot water heater reside along with an awful lot of cartons with her accumulations, stored until I get around to cleaning them out, is dry and comparatively clean.

So it was with more than a sense of surprise that I discovered, when I went down to that basement to bring up a bottle of tomato juice, that there was a puddle on the floor. More than that, there was a cool breeze coming from an open window.

The basement is three-quarters underground. The windows, horizontal rectangles that open from the top, are generally kept closed unless we decide to air out the basement while we're home. Having a husband who is a cop means that you never leave anything open when you go out. However trustful I may be, and I'm not *that* trustful, it's too much for him. He is always on guard against an enemy that may be lurking nearby, perhaps in the vegetable garden.

For the last several years our weather seems to have lurched from drought to flood and back again. In the spring we get drenched. In the summer we get roasted and the nearby reservoir cooks away to practically nothing, forcing us to be even more careful with our water use than usual. It seems terribly unfair that in the spring the reservoir overflows and in the fall we can't water our lawns, but that's the way it is and will be until someone in government does something productive to improve the situation. We may have to wait a good while for that to happen.

On the day that I went downstairs for the bottle of juice, we were recovering from a torrential rain with winds that had knocked down big old trees and scattered debris every which way. Although I had a momentary scare that someone had actually gotten into the basement by opening the window, I realized pretty quickly that I had probably neglected to fasten the window tightly a week or so ago and the wind had blown it open, allowing the rain to come

in. Accepting this explanation was certainly more satis-
fying than imagining that we suddenly had a problem of
underground water rising through the concrete floor.

But the result was the same: I had water in the basement
and a few cartons, probably filled with papers, sitting in
water. I dashed upstairs to get a mop and bucket and set to
work making the floor puddle-free. The problem, of
course, was what to do about the three cartons that had
been sitting in water. They were almost impossible to lift,
as the bottoms were soggy and tended to drop out, but I did
manage to push them to a dry area where I hoped the contents would not mold. I knew I had a job ahead of me. I
would now have to go through them, divide the contents
into Save and Don't Save, and put the stuff I was keeping
into dry cartons.

I didn't look forward to it. Aunt Meg saved things that
had meaning to her: theater programs, tickets torn in half,
old wallets containing even older snapshots, address
books from fifty years ago, receipts for objects purchased
before I was born, and other such memorabilia that put me
in a terrible quandary. What do I do with a photo of an
unidentified person who was dear to my aunt but unknown
to me?

Anyway, the job had to be done and it had to be done by
me. And I knew I ought to do it soon. There was a chance
that the wet material at the bottom of the cartons would not
just mold but smell, and I didn't want to let that happen. I
squeezed out the mop for the last time and thought about
when I could come down here while Eddie, my almost-
four-year-old, would not be around.

And that was how I came across a murder.

1

Eddie loves nursery school. The first year he went, he attended on Tuesdays and Thursdays. This year he goes every Monday, Wednesday, and Friday morning. As it happens, this is very convenient for me, because I have made a great change in my life.

From the time I left St. Stephen's Convent, having been released from my vows, and came to live in the house I inherited from Aunt Meg in Oakwood, New York, I had taught a college course in poetry. Sometime last year I decided that both my students and I would benefit if I taught something new. The college was acquiescent and agreed to let me teach a course on American mysteries by female writers. It seemed an appropriate topic, as I have worked to solve several murders over the last few years.

The best thing about it was that I spent the summer reading the most wonderful books, telling myself it was work and not fun and never believing it for one second. By the end of August I had a syllabus ready, and I began teaching just after Labor Day. It's a Wednesday morning class and Eddie is in nursery school that day, so the changes in both our schedules have meshed nicely.

Nursery school has given Eddie friends who live farther than our neighbors. At the end of September he was invited to a birthday party for a boy who was turning four.

We went to a toy store together, perhaps not the best idea I've ever had, and bought his friend something that I'm sure Eddie wanted for himself, so I made a note of it, as his birthday will be coming along later this fall.

The party was on a Wednesday afternoon, which was no problem. My class ended before lunch and at four we drove over to Ryan Damon's house, where Ryan's mother was preparing a splendid barbecue that included mothers as well as children. The children donned party hats and blew noisemakers, making all of us over the age of four a little crazy, but they had a great time playing a bunch of games and then eating hot dogs and hamburgers and potato chips while we older folks were presented with steaks. I had a feeling as I was eating this wonderful fare that the present should have gone to Ryan's mother.

A large birthday cake, decorated with blue roses and green leaves and lots of butter cream, ended our feast. Every small face was sticky with white stuff and no one wanted to go home. There was something lovely about sitting outside on a lazy autumn evening, breathing in the good fresh air, and knowing it would all end soon, the pleasant weather, the light in the early evening, the leaves still on the trees. Finally, several of us got up and started clearing away the debris and then coaxed our rambunctious youngsters to go home.

"I like Ryan," Eddie said as I seat-belted him in the car.

"He has a very nice mommy, too," I said, appreciating all her hard work.

"I like that cake."

"Well, you have a birthday coming up in a couple of months. We can try to get a cake like that for you."

"And hot dogs."

"But not outside, honey. It'll be too cold by then. We'll do something else. And we'll be sure to invite Ryan."

"OK."

Jack was home by the time we got there. Jack is one husband it's OK to leave without dinner already prepared, as he is the better cook. Eddie told him about every mouthful he had eaten and all the games the kids had played. When he was thoroughly worn out, he went upstairs for a much-needed bath and bed.

Jack had the coffee going when I came downstairs, and we had just settled down to a quiet evening when there was a cry from upstairs. It was the beginning of the worst night of my life.

I won't go into details. Suffice it to say that Eddie was sick and the cause was most likely something he had eaten. Since he had never been this sick before, I was frightened. We decided rather quickly to get him to the emergency room, a first for me, and I hope there will never be a second time. We wrapped him up, grabbed a basin, and tore out of the house.

As we entered the hospital, Jack carrying our very sick child, I heard the woman behind the admissions counter say, "Here comes another one."

Some very capable people immediately took Eddie, who was crying softly, probably because he had lost the energy to do it any louder, to a room where they laid him down and began to work on him. That did provoke some louder cries, but Jack and I had followed closely and we shushed him, holding his hand and talking to him quietly. That I was even able to sound calm and reassuring was something close to a miracle. All I could think of was E. coli and salmonella, two terms that struck absolute terror inside me.

Jack started asking questions, as two of us could not stand near enough to comfort Eddie. Eddie was the third child to be brought in and they were anticipating more, considering the number of children at the party. No adults had been stricken, at least not so far.

I tossed out that the mothers had eaten steak and the children had been given different fare.

"Have a good time at the party, Eddie?" the doctor asked.

Eddie stopped crying and blinked. He said a soft, "Yes," and sniffled.

"What did you eat?"

"A hot dog."

"That's all?"

"A hamburger." He screeched as a needle pricked him.

"You're doing fine," the doctor said. "You're a pretty brave kid, you know that?"

Eddie nodded and I smiled.

"So that was all you ate? A hot dog and a hamburger? I bet you had some ice cream and cake, too."

"Uh-huh."

"Anything else?"

" 'Tato salad and 'tato chips."

"Potato salad. Hey, that sounds good. Wish I'd been at that party."

Bet you don't, I said to myself, all the while admiring his skill in moving fast and talking at the same time. "There was coleslaw on the table, too," I said, trying to remember. "I'm very concerned about E. coli."

"We don't think it's E. coli," the doctor said. "But whatever it was, it was something the kids ate and not the mothers, so it could be the franks or hamburgers."

"Have you talked to the woman who prepared the party?" Jack asked.

"Mrs. Damon. Yes. We have someone going over the details with her right now and we're bringing in the Department of Health. We'll get to the bottom of this, but it may not happen tonight." He raised his head and looked at me.

"Maybe you'd like to sit down, Mrs. Brooks. You're looking a little worse than your son right now, and I don't want
another patient on my hands."

I tried for a smile, but he was right. My fear had gotten
the better of me, wearing me out. When Jack shoved a
chair under my bottom, I sat down gratefully.

Three more children were brought in in the next hour,
one of them Ryan, the birthday boy. Pat Damon was beside
herself. The hamburger meat had been freshly bought that
day, also the hot dogs. The birthday cake came from everybody's favorite bakery. The ice cream went from the store
freezer to her freezer at home. The salads were from an upscale delicatessen. *This could not have happened.* She was
so apologetic, I finally told her to stop. It wasn't her fault
and I felt sure that between the hospital and the Department of Health, the source would be determined.

The doctor decided to keep all six children overnight,
and I spent the night sitting in Eddie's room, listening to
him breathe, watching his face, touching his skin, and
trying not to cry. Jack stayed with me most of that time,
but during the night he went to the rooms of the other little
children and talked to their anxious parents. The con-
sensus was that it had to be the chopped meat or the franks,
as those were the two foods none of the mothers tasted.

But not all the sick children had eaten the same things.
One child had eaten half a hot dog and no hamburger and
one had eaten only a hamburger and no hot dog. Every
child had had at least some cake, but I had had cake, too,
and I was feeling fine, or at least my digestive system was.
And not all the children at the party had been afflicted.

About two in the morning Jack suggested I lie down on
the cot that was there for that purpose, but I refused. I was
so filled with terror, so shaken at the fragility of my child
and all the others, I could not leave his bedside. At some

point I did doze off in the chair, and I was glad, when I awoke, that I had gotten some sleep, as I would be taking Eddie home in the morning and I didn't want to pass out or something stupid like that when I was alone with him.

Jack offered to stay home, but I felt he should go to work as usual. The only one of the three of us who got a good night's sleep, as it turned out, was Eddie. I kissed Jack and held him rather dramatically, then let him go. At the hospital, they checked Eddie out, fed him soft food, kept him for a while after that, and then let me take him home. Several other mothers were doing the same, and we exchanged greetings and gossip. No one in the hospital admitted to knowing what had caused the poisoning.

I talked to several of the mothers during the day, including Pat Damon, who could not stop apologizing. She had been interviewed by the Department of Health in the morning and she had turned over the receipts for the food she had bought, most of which were still in the bottom of the bags she had taken it home in, ready to be reused or recycled. She had also handed over samples of all the food that was left. Not one mother had gotten sick, and three children, who were also being interviewed, had also not gotten sick. It was quite a mystery.

After lunch, I took a greatly needed nap while Eddie did the same. I awoke feeling much more human and was gratified to see that Eddie's color was returning to his cheeks. I decided to keep him home from nursery school the next day so he could continue to recover until Monday, when I hoped he would be well enough to go back. Considering the horror of the previous night, that Thursday was quite calm and restored my confidence. Jack called several times, and when he came home he was carrying a toy for Eddie. I think that did more to make us all feel better than anything else.

Eddie improved steadily over the next several days and by Monday morning was anxious to go to nursery school. I knew from the grapevine that the other afflicted children were also going back, and by that time I think we were all confident that whatever had caused the affliction, it was out of everyone's system for good.

With Eddie out of the house for a few hours, I decided the time had come to go down to the basement and get to work on the cartons that had been soaked a week earlier.

2

I carried a flattened carton down the basement stairs with me, knowing that however hard I tried to dispose of the contents of the three wet boxes, I would not succeed. Sometimes there are advantages to being a realist.

I took the nearest carton, sat on an old folding chair, and bent over to untie the cord that bound it. The top of the carton was bone-dry, as were the contents on top, probably, I thought, going right down to the near-bottom. I think my aunt lived in a perpetual state of fear that some agency of the government would come to her for documents from her past, even those that had long ago expired. In a medium-sized brown envelope were insurance papers on the life of my Uncle Will, who died several years before Aunt Meg. I put those in a supermarket bag I had brought down for things I would dispose of. There were also bankbooks from the 1970s and earlier in Margaret's name and Will's. Believe it or not, there were sales receipts for clothing Aunt Meg had bought at local stores and department stores, all of which had been paid for at least seven years ago, according to the dates, and perhaps longer. I am sure that the purchases had long since found their way to the Salvation Army or some other worthy charity. There were moments when I chided my aunt out loud, other moments when I just laughed.

To my absolute delight, I found when I got down to the

wet and icky stuff that there was nothing in this carton that anyone in his right mind would save one more minute. I retied the cord and left the carton for Jack to carry upstairs to be disposed of on our next garbage collection day.

Thrilled with my success, I dragged over carton number two. This one was not tied. Instead, the four top flaps were interleaved to keep it closed. I pulled them open and started my way down.

This collection of material was more memorabilia than financial documents and therefore much more interesting to me. Nice and dry on top were a few old photograph albums that appeared to date from my aunt's childhood. They had stiff board covers and black pages filled with black-and-white snapshots pasted in with triangular corner holders. I flipped a few pages, marveling at the children whom I knew only as adults, then closed it and set it aside. Unlike the contents of the last carton, these things were treasures, and I would handle them as such.

I dug deeper, carefully stacking loose pictures and envelopes of photos and newspaper clippings, many of them about events that happened before I was born. About halfway down, I found a black-and-white marbled notebook of the kind that schoolchildren use, or used to many years ago. I opened it and found it was a kind of journal written by my aunt. The entries were not made daily or even weekly, although sometimes they were. Each one was dated and events or personal thoughts were recorded, sometimes in full sentences, sometimes just in phrases. I read some and was sorry I had. This volume had been written during that terrible year that Gene, my aunt and uncle's only child, had been ill and, to complicate matters, I was living with them, as my mother had died. I could sense Aunt Meg's misery and anxiety. She had choices to make that year that would have been difficult in the best of circumstances, and these were the worst.

Lower down in the carton were more journals, some written in similar schoolbooks, some in fancier notebooks, probably gifts from people who knew Aunt Meg enjoyed writing. A glance at each one was all I allowed myself. Time was running short and I wanted to get as much of this task done as possible before Eddie came home. I picked up one item after another, made a judgment, and put it in the dry carton I had brought from upstairs.

After several journals and envelopes of snapshots that had not yet been pasted into albums, I found a small envelope, hand-addressed to my aunt. I opened it and began to read the letter inside.

Dear Mrs. Wirth,
    I cannot thank you enough for helping me through this terrible time. I don't know what I would have done without you. My grief is nearly unbearable. Thank you for your kindness, your warmth, your understanding. I will never forget you.
Sincerely,
Betty Linton

The name meant nothing to me, but I saved the note. There was an envelope right underneath it, also hand-addressed, and I pulled out the letter inside.

Dear Meg,
    I saw you at the funeral but didn't get a chance to speak to you. I know how fond you were of Darby and I understand what a personal loss this must be to you. You always treated him as though he were your own. I'm sure Gene will miss him as well.
    If I can be of any help, please call. If you just want to talk or complain to a sympathetic ear—I know you never

complain, but maybe you should once in a while—I am here. I will not be embarrassed by tears, dear.

This has been such a terrible time what with all the other things that have been happening. God bless you. I think of you often.

The note was signed *Celia*, with no last name. I could not recall a Celia in my aunt's life, but that didn't mean anything. After I went to live at St. Stephen's, I didn't see a lot of my aunt for several years until I began, as an adult, to drive down to Oakwood once a month to visit her and Gene.

I thought, however, that the name Darby rang a faint bell. I put the letter back in its envelope and the envelope in the fresh carton, then picked up the next item in the old carton. It was a memorial card for the funeral of Darby Maxwell, who died at the age of twenty-two. The card showed a traditional picture of Jesus on one side and Darby's name, the date of his death, and the Lord's Prayer on the other. I saved the card and continued my search.

Paper-clipped together were several yellowing newspaper clippings. The top one was a small obituary for Darby Maxwell. Darby had died "an accidental death" while on a trip away from his home, which was Greenwillow. That, of course, gave me the connection. Greenwillow is the residence for retarded adults that my cousin Gene has lived in for many years. I glanced at my watch, took the memorial card with me, and went upstairs. There I called Greenwillow and asked to talk to the director.

"Chris," she said with obvious pleasure, "how nice to hear from you. I know you slip in and out, but I haven't seen you in months."

"You're always busy, Virginia. Do you have a minute now?"

"Absolutely."

"I want to ask you about someone who I think was a resident some years ago. His name was Darby Maxwell."

"Darby. Yes, of course. Poor Darby. What a terrible story that was."

"I take it he died."

"Yes, and we were all brokenhearted."

"Did my cousin know him?"

"They were best friends, Chris. They were close in age and they liked many of the same things. They were frequently together. Gene was devastated when Darby didn't come back."

"And my aunt," I went on. "Was she close to Darby, too?"

"Very close. Darby's mother had moved away—she had remarried. I remember that we talked about it, whether she should move him to another facility closer to where she lived. I thought moving him would be a mistake. His friends were here; he had lived here for several years. After she left, your aunt really filled in as a second mother. She would pick both young men up and take them to church. She would have them home for Sunday dinner. I don't mean to say that Darby's mother didn't visit and watch over him, but her visits were somewhat limited." Virginia McAlpine is a woman who dislikes criticizing others.

"If I drop over this afternoon, would you tell me about Darby's death? It's almost time for my son to come home from nursery school right now."

"I'll be in today and I'll look forward to your visit. Can you tell me why you're suddenly interested in something that happened so many years ago?"

I told her about my digging through Aunt Margaret's things. "I found some notes thanking her for her help and kindness when Darby died. It's something about my aunt that I didn't know. She obviously did many good things in her life besides caring for me, and she kept all these things to herself. It's a whole side of her I know nothing about."

"It will be my pleasure to tell you the story."

We got over there about three o'clock. Gene was playing a game with a friend, but as soon as he saw us he came over. He and Eddie get along just fine, and I left them in the activities area and went to Virginia's office. We exchanged greetings, talked for a few minutes about Gene, and then got down to the story of Darby Maxwell.

"Darby was a little younger than Gene, I think," she began, "but they got along wonderfully. His parents divorced when Darby was fairly young and after Darby came to live in Greenwillow—that was at the old location, of course—Mrs. Maxwell remarried and became Mrs. Linton. For her, it was a new life. Her first husband had left her because of Darby. It was a situation he just couldn't handle. She was a devoted mother and visited probably once a month, less than she would have liked, but it was quite a drive for her to get here.

"Darby always visited her in Connecticut for two weeks in the summer or fall and usually went to her for Christmas, as I remember. The tragedy happened during one of those fall visits. All I can tell you is what I heard and read in the news reports. Darby and his mother went to visit friends, people who lived in a country house with a lot of space out back. The property bordered on woods. The story is that Darby and his friend, who was not retarded, went out back and walked into the woods. Somehow, Darby got away from his friend and was lost.

"They didn't find him for many days, although I know that a search was organized that same day. There was a pond somewhere in all that land and they dragged it, looking for him. The weather turned bad a couple of days after he disappeared. It rained very heavily, it got cold at night as it sometimes does in September, and the experts began to despair of finding him alive. When they finally did find him, it was in a place they had passed before, several times, in fact. So he must have been alive during that part of the search. It was very sad. Gene was distraught; I can tell you that."

"That really is a terrible story," I said. "Was the funeral around here?"

"Yes. Mrs. Linton felt that his friends should be able to attend and we all did. She went to her old church, not here in Oakwood but nearby. He was buried in Connecticut."

"What part did my aunt play in all this?"

"She helped Mrs. Linton make the arrangements. I believe she even had her stay at her home for a couple of nights. Your aunt felt she had lost one of her own, but the truth is, she would have done it for anyone here; she was that kind of person."

"That's very kind of you to say. She never told me about this. I suppose it must have happened ten or twelve years ago."

"About that, yes. I could look up the date."

"I have some clippings in an old carton," I said. "I'm sure the date is on one of them. Not that it matters. I really wanted to know what Margaret's part was in all this."

"She was more than helpful."

"Would you mind if I talked to Gene about Darby?"

"I don't think there's any harm. I'm sure he'll remember. He has a good memory for things that are important to him."

That was certainly true. "Thank you, Virginia. It's been good talking to you."

I left her to her work and went out to find my son and my cousin. They were giggling together, some of Gene's beloved miniature cars on the floor between them. I watched from a distance, happy that my son accepted

Gene and that Gene got along well with Eddie. When there was a lull, I walked over and sat down on the floor with them. I talked to Gene for a minute or two, checking as I always did to make sure he was getting along well, eating well, and enjoying his life. Eddie played by himself with the cars as we talked.

Finally I said, "Gene, do you remember Darby?"

"My friend Darby?" he said.

"Yes."

"Darby died. I cried and cried. He was my friend."

"Did your mama know Darby?"

"Uh-huh."

"Did Darby go to your house sometimes?"

"Uh-huh. He came for dinner. Mama made dinner."

"He must have been a very nice boy," I said.

"He was. He was my best friend. He went away and died."

"I'm glad you remember him." I patted Gene on the back. We are almost exactly the same age, and I reflect sometimes on how I grew from a girl to a woman while Gene's body became that of a man while his personality remained that of a sweet child. In a few years Eddie will have outgrown him intellectually, but I hope they stay friends forever, as Gene and I have.

We stayed a little while longer; then Eddie and I went home to get dinner ready and wait for Jack to come home. Later in the evening, after Eddie was asleep, I told Jack about my basement cleanup and where it had led me. As always, I was sorry Jack and Aunt Meg had never met. They were each part of a different segment of my life.

3

I heard nothing more about the mysterious bug that had attacked the children at Ryan's birthday party. I called Pat, his mother, but she had no answers, and I called the hospital, but the people I talked to seemed confused and weren't sure what I was talking about. I didn't think that was a very good sign, but I told myself that everyone nowadays is overworked and since no one had been seriously injured, perhaps they were taking the incident less seriously than we mothers.

It wasn't till Friday of that week that I got back to the cartons in the basement. I had left them in such a way that I could pick up exactly where I had left off. I continued digging in the old, mildewing carton, taking out a handful of things that were next in line for a decision. To my surprise, I was immediately confronted with another death.

It was at that moment that it registered in my brain what the mysterious Celia had meant in the letter she had written Aunt Meg after Darby's funeral. She had referred to all the terrible things that had happened and perhaps it was this second funeral—or rather, this first one, as I was reading in reverse chronological order—that she had meant.

Again there was a holy card, this one with the name of Lawrence Norton Filmore, who had died at the age of fifty. The obituary in the local paper contained a photograph of a good-looking man with a mustache over a happy smile. The copy extended to two columns and detailed a life of work, family, and philanthropy. It appeared that he had lived right here in Oakwood and his funeral was at the church that Aunt Meg attended, as well as Jack, Eddie, and I. The address in the paper was a mile or so from where we lived, but I didn't recall Aunt Meg ever mentioning him to me.

The startling thing about the obituary was in the second paragraph: "The cause of death was an apparent suicide." Suicide is a very delicate situation in the Catholic Church. Traditionally, victims of suicide were not allowed a Catholic funeral. In recent times, however, a more generous approach to suicide has come about. Although taking one's life is a sin, it is thought that the victim may have had doubts about his act at a moment when it was too late to go back, such as after the finger pulled the trigger. Looked at that way, the victim can be forgiven, and nowadays many suicides are given Catholic funerals and buried in hallowed ground. This was apparently one of those cases, as the church was mentioned in the article.

Another newspaper clipping, this one written several days before the obituary, talked about the disappearance of Mr. Filmore just after a large party given in celebration of his birthday. Almost four hundred people had attended, and from the description, it sounded like quite a bash. I looked at the next items in the carton, and sure enough, there was an invitation to Aunt Meg for the party. "You are invited to the Happy Birthday Party for Larry Filmore," the text said. "Please help us celebrate half a century of the life of a great man. No presents will be accepted. Instead, please give a donation to a favorite charity or one of the following." Three organizations were mentioned, one of them a special fund at the church.

Yet another newspaper article appeared to have been published a day or two after the big birthday party, giving names of prominent guests, the menu, the band, and a description of the decorations, which sounded lovely. I could only imagine the surprise and shock of the family after the object of this grand celebration took his life. Even today, I thought, they must still be wondering why.

I rummaged through the papers nearby and found a note from Laura Filmore thanking Margaret for her kindness, etc., after Larry died. What a time my aunt must have had, I thought, two deaths in such a short period of time, two people she was deeply fond of. I was curious about this suicide but knew I couldn't ask Melanie Gross, my closest friend in town, as she hadn't lived here a dozen years ago. I looked at my watch, saw I had some time before Eddie's nursery school ended, and gathered together the documents concerning Lawrence Filmore. I took them upstairs and called my next-door neighbor, Midge McDonald, who has lived here much longer than I. She was home and invited me over for a cup of coffee. Armed with my papers, I went.

Midge is a very cheerful woman who married young, by which I mean in her early twenties, and now has a teenager and two children approaching their teens. She is one of those people who always seem to be busy, and I had been surprised to find her at home. Her house is to the left of ours as you face them, one of the older homes on the street. Beyond our house on the other side are houses built in a newer style at a later time.

By the time I got to her door, the coffee was already dripping into a filter paper and filling the air with a wonderful fragrance. On the kitchen table were two ceramic cups and saucers in bright colors as well as matching sugar and creamer in the center of the table.

"It's great to see you, Chris," she said. "Sometimes I

think we pass in the night. I haven't set eyes on you for weeks."

"I've been doing a bunch of word processing for my lawyer friend in New York and I'm teaching a new course this semester, so I've been doing a lot of reading for it."

"That's wonderful. I wish I could teach."

"You do plenty of other things."

"I guess we all do. What's all that stuff?" She was looking at my rubber-banded bunch of papers from the basement.

"I was wondering if you remembered a man named Lawrence Filmore. He died about a dozen years ago and I think you lived here then."

"I sure do," she said, sliding into the chair opposite mine. "He committed suicide, Chris. The circumstances were very strange."

"What do you mean?"

"Well, I didn't know him personally, but your aunt did. I remember talking to her about it afterward. He had some big birthday, fifty or sixty, and disappeared the next morning. No one had any idea where he was for days and then he was found dead. He had shot himself."

"That certainly is unusual."

"No one who knew him could believe it. This was a happy man, a well-to-do man, a man with a great family and a million friends. And they had all turned out to honor him and then this happened."

"It must have been a real shock."

"Your aunt couldn't believe it. She used to talk about it years after it happened. Nobody knew why he had done it. You would think if something were wrong in his business, the problem would turn up eventually. But it didn't. Or at least, I never heard anything."

"I suppose he could have been clinically depressed," I said.

"Lots of people are. But he seemed like a happy man."

"Was my aunt a personal friend?"

"She said she had eaten at their home on a number of occasions. I think she worked on some of his philanthropic projects. And she knew them well enough that she was invited to the big party. What makes you interested in this? You didn't know him yourself, did you?"

I told her about my basement escapade. Then we talked about other things, the school, the construction on some of the streets, a teacher her son was having difficulty with. We each drank a second cup of coffee and I admired her cups and saucers. They had come from the Southwest, where her parents were now living.

I was getting ready to go when Midge said, "Someone else died at about that time. I can't quite remember the details, but I know it upset Meg a great deal, especially coming just after Mr. Filmore's death."

I told her what I knew of Darby Maxwell, and as I related the circumstances of his death she nodded.

"Yes, that's what Meg was so troubled about, that young man that was a friend of her son. She grieved for him as though she had been his mother."

"It's strange she didn't mention it to me," I said. "I came down every month. I guess he must have died in between visits and she didn't want to upset me. Although now I think about it, she did say something, but not as emotionally as you've described."

"Believe me, she was very troubled. As I recall, she said he had wandered away from the family and was found a week later, dead of exposure."

"That's what these newspaper clippings say. Tell me, do you know anyone named Celia here in town?"

"Celia. Let's see. I think the former mayor's wife was named Celia."

"That could be the person. There's a lovely note to my aunt from a woman of that name, but there's no return address and no last name."

Midge looked at me through narrowed eyes. "You don't think these deaths were murders, do you?"

"Not at all," I said, laughing. My neighbors know what I've been doing these past few years, solving murders both locally and in some other places, so I could understand why she was suspicious. "I was just interested because it's a side of my aunt that I didn't know. She was a great person and was obviously involved in a lot more good things than she let on."

"She sure was. I think of her a lot, Chris. She would have loved to meet your husband and see your Eddie."

Just what I had thought. "Well, I thank you for your time. It's almost time for Eddie to come home."

"Drop over anytime. I've enjoyed talking to you."

That was the end of my inquiries, or I thought it was. At night, I told Jack what I had learned. The suicide intrigued him more than Darby's death, which he attributed to Darby's inability to find his way back, thus becoming the victim of the outdoor weather. But the suicide of a well-loved man whose entire life appeared to be in order gave him an uncomfortable feeling.

"Of course, I think we often ask *why?* when we're dealing with a suicide. Even people whose lives aren't in order, who have money problems or emotional problems, can find help if they just say something."

"They're embarrassed," I said. "Or frightened. Or uninformed. There are lots of reasons for keeping quiet. You think I should ask some questions?"

"Far be it from me to tell you not to, but it's a long time ago and families of suicides don't like to talk about it. I don't think you'll get anywhere."

"Well, I'll save the papers. If nothing else, they say something about my aunt."

The course I was teaching on Wednesday mornings had given me the opportunity to go back and read or reread old favorite mysteries. I found myself enjoying Dorothy Sayers immensely. My problem was, when I got into one series, I hated to leave it for another, even though I was trying to read chronologically and make sense out of the development of the mystery genre. My notes became as thick as the manuscript for a book as I analyzed book after book, author after author. There was no question of reading everything Rex Stout or Agatha Christie had written; I'd have been at it forever. But I had read a good many of their books when I was a nun—mysteries were favorite reading at St. Stephen's—so I was ahead of the game.

I stopped thinking about the unhappy deaths of a dozen years ago and concentrated on the present, preparing for my next class. But something happened to bring it all back to me. Several days after my coffee with Midge, the phone rang and a woman introduced herself as Celia Yaeger.

"I ran into your neighbor Midge McDonald yesterday," the voice said. "She said you wanted to talk to me."

"Oh," I said in surprise. "Mrs. Yaeger. I believe you knew my aunt, Margaret Wirth."

"I knew her very well, a lovely, wonderful person. I miss her in my life today even though she's been gone for several years." She spoke in a careful, well-modulated voice. I could imagine her presiding over a meeting or conference, everything in perfect order.

"I found a note from you among my aunt's possessions," I said. "It was written after Mr. Filmore died some years ago."

"I'm sure I did write to her then. She had worked with him on at least one project and she was very helpful after he died, getting papers together, seeing to it that his good work wouldn't be lost. And it happened at a terrible time. There was another death, too."

"Darby Maxwell."

"Yes, that was his name, a resident of Greenwillow. You must know about Greenwillow. Margaret's son lives there."

"We're very close," I said.

"I'm glad to hear it. What was it you wanted to ask me?"

I felt a little embarrassed. I didn't really want to ask her anything. Midge must have misunderstood. "I was just interested in Aunt Meg's involvement with those two people. She never talked about them."

"Your aunt was a modest person, Mrs. Brooks. I don't think I ever heard her toot her own horn in all the years I knew her. She probably didn't know how. But she tooted everybody else's; I can tell you that."

"That's very kind of you." I wasn't sure what to say and I felt awkward. "Well, I thank you for calling."

"Why don't we have lunch? I don't think I've ever met you and you've lived here some time now. Can you make it tomorrow?"

I told her I could if we made it at twelve-thirty, as I was teaching, and she said that would be fine. When I got off the phone, I called Elsie Rivers, Eddie's surrogate grandmother, and arranged for him to spend the second half of his day with her.

Then I tried to think of what Mrs. Yaeger and I would talk about.

4

I dressed for class on Wednesday morning. I'm a bit more formal than some of the teachers, who come in wearing torn jeans and flannel shirts. I generally wear a skirt with a blouse or sweater, sometimes a jacket. Mrs. Yaeger had sounded more like my mother's generation than my own, so I surmised she would appreciate some formality. I didn't know what to expect when I parked in front of her house after I drove back from my class. Fictional killers and sleuths were swirling in my head as they tended to do when I finished teaching.

The house was one of the older ones in Oakwood, and I could see where it had been extended as so many, including ours, have. I rang the bell and a small, thin, gray-haired woman opened the door, grasped my hand firmly with enthusiasm, gave me a welcoming smile, and invited me inside.

"Would you care to join me in a glass of sherry?" she asked when my coat had been hung in the hall closet.

"That would be very nice." I'm not much of a drinker, but I thought I could manage some sherry without falling asleep at the table.

We sat in the living room with our drinks and a platter of canapés that included thin slices of cucumber with notched edges, blue cheese, and rice crackers and some others that were less identifiable but very tasty.

"When my husband was mayor, I tried to meet as many families as I could," my hostess said, "but I know I've missed a lot of newcomers in the last few years. I knew you'd moved in after Meg died, but I never got to meet you."

"It's a pleasure to be here. I see you're a very good cook."

"I've had many years to practice," she said matter-of-factly. "I assume you're the nun Meg talked about."

"I was, yes. I was released from my vows the spring my aunt died. She left the house to me and I thought I'd try out living here. I now have a husband and a son and we're very happy in Oakwood."

"I'm glad to hear it. I've heard a bit about you. You were influential in moving Greenwillow into town."

"That happened the first summer I lived here. It's made it very nice for me. I'm able to see Gene, my cousin, whenever I want."

"That other death we talked about on the phone was his friend. It was very sad, a young man with many people who loved him, a victim of the elements."

"My cousin remembers him very well." I reached for what seemed to be a piece of shrimp on a triangle of toast, wondering if I would ever have the patience to create a batch of these lovely little appetizers. "Did you know either of the men who died?" I asked.

"I didn't know the one at Greenwillow—they weren't in town at that time, as you know—but I knew Larry Filmore quite well. He was a dear man, a hard worker, very generous with his money."

"His suicide must have shocked everyone who knew him."

"It most certainly did." She set her empty sherry glass on the table. "Shall we go into the dining room?"

I followed her. A polished table was set for two on elegant place mats. Elaborate silver serving pieces lay on the table, and crystal glasses were at each place. I hadn't counted on more wine with lunch, and I wondered how I would tolerate it. A beautiful salad was at each place, a roll on each bread-and-butter plate. Mrs. Yaeger poured white wine without asking, and I tasted mine as Jack had taught me to, inhaling the aroma first. I was sure it was a fine wine.

"Yes, Larry's suicide left us all reeling," she said, picking up the thread from the living room. "Why does a man do such a thing? Why does anyone do it, but especially a man who had so much to live for? We'll never know."

"There was nothing suspicious about it?"

"Everything was suspicious. Where did he go in the wee hours after his birthday party? Why did he leave the house? Where did he spend the time?"

"Are there any answers?"

"None that I know of. He left mysteriously; he came back mysteriously."

"Does his wife still live in town?"

"Yes, Laura's still in the house. She has many friends and a full life, but that broken heart will never mend."

"I assume the police did an investigation."

"As far as I know. They had a fair idea how far he had driven, but he never got gas while he was away and never charged a toll or anything else, so they don't know where he went. And he wasn't sighted."

"Was he shot?"

"Yes, by his own hand."

"Was it his gun?"

"I don't remember now," she said, breaking her roll and buttering half. "Laura would know."

I wondered if that meant Lawrence Filmore had owned a gun. "You wrote a very lovely note to my aunt," I said,

changing the subject somewhat. "It was filled with kindness and warmth. I'm sure she appreciated it. I found it last
week in a carton in the basement and I asked Midge if she
knew someone named Celia."

She smiled. "That puts all the pieces in place. Tell me
about yourself, Christine. You've certainly had an interesting and unusual background."

I went through it all as we ate our lunch. She was a
pleasant woman who clearly tried to make me feel appreciated. I thought she must have been a tremendous asset to
her husband while he was mayor, but that was before I
moved to Oakwood, and Meg had never mentioned either
one of them.

When I left, after a homemade dessert and very good
coffee, I felt as though I had a new friend.

That evening, when I next had some free time, I flipped
through Aunt Meg's journals, reading an entry here and
there but not devoting a lot of time to it. These I would
keep. They were her thoughts, her feelings, her concerns,
her pleasures, and her griefs. I found the book that corre-
sponded in time to the two deaths I had learned about, and
in that one I searched for the entries in which she wrote
about them. I didn't learn much more than I had from
Midge, Celia, Virginia McAlpine, and the newspaper clippings. When I was done, I set it all aside and got to work on
next week's class.

I woke up on Thursday morning thinking about Darby
Maxwell and his mother. After breakfast, I decided to call
her, just to introduce myself and tell her my connection to
her family. Virginia at Greenwillow gave me the last phone
number she had, already a dozen years old, and I called.

"You must be the nun," she said when I told her I was
Meg's niece.

"I was when you knew my aunt. I'm living in her house now." I went on to explain the details and we talked for about ten minutes. She sounded very much like my aunt in some ways, and I enjoyed listening to her voice.

Finally, she said, "If you're in Oakwood, you're not all that far from where we live in Connecticut. Would you like to come up and visit?"

I hadn't planned anything beyond the phone call and it took me a moment to answer, during which she pressed me to come. She would like to see me for lunch tomorrow, nothing fancy—"I'm not a fancy person," she said—just good, plain food. I have to say that was very appealing, as I am a lover of good, plain food. I said yes, made my arrangements with Elsie, and felt rather pleased that I would be spending a few hours with someone who reminded me of Aunt Meg.

We live on the Long Island Sound, a body of water between the north shore of Long Island, which juts into the Atlantic Ocean, and the northeast coast of New York State and the southern coast of Connecticut, which are contiguous. As you travel north and east along this coast, the sound eventually gives way to the Atlantic.

Betty Linton lived north of the coast, somewhere in the middle of Connecticut, more or less on the way to Massachusetts. Jack and I looked at a map that evening and figured out the best way for me to go. It was fall and likely to be a very beautiful drive, with the leaves turning but not yet falling.

I got Eddie off to nursery school and told him Elsie would pick him up and I would be home later in the afternoon.

"Where are you going?" he asked.

"I'm visiting a lady in Connecticut."

"Is she a nice lady?"

"I think she is."

The drive was as pleasant as I had anticipated. When I finally reached the house I was looking for, I was surprised to find an old, well-cared-for wooden structure on several acres of land. The old-fashioned mailbox at the road said: LINTON and I went up a long drive and parked. I estimated the house to have been built in the middle of the nineteenth century, and many of the trees around it must have been at least that old. It was quite lovely.

Mrs. Linton came out of the front door with a smile and a wave after I got out of the car. I think I loved her at first sight. There was a resemblance to my aunt, not so much in looks but in spirit. She was spry and energetic, with an easy smile.

"You don't look a bit like your aunt," she said, offering her hand, "but it's a pleasure to meet you. I know that you're Gene's cousin. He always talked about you."

"He used to call me 'the brown lady' because the Franciscan habit I wore was brown."

"Come inside. You've had a long drive and it's chilly out here."

The inside of the house was wonderful, lots of old wood beams, floors that were surely original and well polished. The Lintons had obviously gone to great pains to furnish the house with American antiques. There were oil lamps of great beauty that had been converted to electricity, an old hand-carved baby's rocker, and handwoven rugs. It was a treasure trove and I wished I had the time to inspect every item.

"We've had a good time filling up this house," Betty Linton said. "It was bare when we moved in, except for a few old things that we eventually threw away. Let's sit down for a while and talk. You can try that rocking chair. It's not an antique, just old. It's the chair my mother sat in with me when I was a baby and fussed. Be careful, dear. It may put you to sleep." She smiled.

It was carved, stained oak and I sat in it gingerly, but it was strong and firm and comfortable, even without a cushion. We talked for about half an hour, then moved into the dining room, where a fire burned in one of many fireplaces. Here there were even more things to admire. A corner cupboard caught my attention, as well as the dishes it held. Mrs. Linton said the cupboard was part of the house, but they had had it refinished. The glass panes in the doors were original and leaded. I looked through one and saw the waviness.

"It really is wonderful having you here," Betty Linton said. "I'm afraid I didn't keep up with your aunt after my son died; it was too painful. But we did talk once or twice a year and I heard from someone when she died; maybe it was from Virginia at Greenwillow."

"I never knew about your son. I just learned about what happened recently, when I got to cleaning out a carton of Meg's papers and found a letter from you and some news clippings. I know it was a long time ago, but I'm very sorry about Darby."

"Thank you. It was twelve years ago, but when I think of it, which is often, it feels as though it happened just last week. He was such a good boy and he died such an unpleasant death. He must have been so frightened, so cold, so frustrated that he couldn't find his way home."

"I talked to Gene about him after I read your letter. He remembers Darby well."

"Thank you," she said, as though I had complimented her.

We ate a hot casserole that bubbled as she brought it to the table. There was no wine, which was fine with me, but we drank our water from pewter cups, which were cold to the touch. I turned down her offer of coffee, and when we were finished she took me outside to see the grounds.

The sun was shining brilliantly and warmed me through

the chill air. There was an old chicken coop on the property, long empty, and a small wooden building that once must have housed a caretaker. It would have made a great place for me to do my word processing and to plan my classes and mark my papers.

About fifty feet away was a pond that Betty said her husband swam in every day of the summer. And all over were flowers and shrubs, and there was even a vegetable garden. Without walking into it, I could see orange pumpkins sitting on the ground amid green leaves and browning stems.

We went back inside and had apple cider and doughnuts in front of the warm fire. I was sorry I hadn't arranged to come when Jack could accompany me; I thought he would have loved to see this house.

"I have a wonderful husband," Betty said as we relaxed. "The first ten years of Darby's life were very difficult, and his father simply couldn't come to terms with a child like Darby. We tried a number of residential institutions, but that only worked until Darby came home for a vacation. And of course, the expense was terrible."

"I know," I said.

"Finally we split up. I met Brad Linton a few years later and he changed my life. I was very lucky. Except, of course, for what happened to Darby."

"Did you meet my aunt through Greenwillow?"

"Through our sons, yes. I didn't live in Oakwood, where your aunt lived. We were farther north. But Meg and I managed to have lunch together from time to time. And when Darby died, she was simply wonderful. I lived up here by then and I stayed at her house, as the funeral was where we used to live instead of here, and she saw to it that I survived. I don't know how else to put it."

"Virginia said she saw a lot of Darby."

"Oh, she did. She'd have both boys to the house for Sunday dinner on weekends when I didn't visit. She'd drop in during the week and sit and talk to them. When I married Brad, we moved up here and my visits were curtailed. His father almost never came," she added sadly.

"I read the clippings about Darby's death. It sounded to me as though everyone turned out to try to find him."

"They did. They walked through the woods all that night, carrying big lanterns and calling his name. If he'd been there, he would have heard. He must have gone far away, just kept walking in the wrong direction till it was too late."

"And circled back," I said.

"Yes. He must have. There was nothing anyone could do. I blame only myself."

"Oh, no," I said. "It wasn't—"

"I shouldn't have let him out of my sight. The young man he was with just didn't understand that the house and grounds were unfamiliar to Darby, that he could be distracted easily, perhaps hearing a bird chirp, or seeing a little chipmunk run through the leaves. I let down my guard and I shouldn't have."

I felt very bad, knowing she lived with this guilt. "It was a terrible accident, Betty. No one was at fault."

She didn't respond. She got up and put a couple of logs on the fire. When she sat down, she said, "There was one strange thing."

"What do you mean?"

"Sometime after Darby died, they gave me back his clothes and the ring he always wore. The sneakers weren't his. They were somebody else's."

5

I felt stunned by her gentle, matter-of-fact comment. "What do you mean?"

"I had helped him tie his laces the morning we went to visit our friends. The sneakers were white and fairly new. The ones they gave back to me were black and much more worn."

"Did you inquire about it?"

"I called the hospital—the morgue is in the hospital—and asked. They said those were the clothes he had been wearing. I spoke to the man who had put them in the bag. For a moment I think he thought I was accusing him of stealing Darby's sneakers, but I made it clear I thought there'd been a mistake. He assured me there hadn't."

"Did you tell the police?"

"I couldn't see any reason to. Darby was gone. He had died of exposure. I was in terrible shape. I could hardly carry on a conversation. I decided he'd found the sneakers somewhere and for some reason put them on."

"Were the laces tied?" I asked, remembering what she had said about tying them for Darby on their last morning.

She took her time answering. "I didn't see them on him," she said. "But after all those days and all he must have endured, I expect his own sneakers wouldn't have been tied anymore."

She was right and I didn't want to pursue this any longer. She was having a hard time maintaining her composure. I dropped the subject and asked if she would show me the house. We took a tour, which I enjoyed very much. When we got downstairs, I asked her if Jack and Eddie and I might visit sometime, and she said she would like that. A little while later, I left.

All I could think of on the ride home was the mystery of the sneakers. Betty had probably been right: Darby had found a pair of old sneakers somewhere and, for whatever reason, perhaps because his were wet, took his off and put on the others. I tried to think how that could have happened. Who leaves a pair of sneakers out-of-doors? Maybe someone by a swimming pool or a pond. One of the clippings had mentioned a lake. But it just didn't seem right to me.

I got back in late afternoon, went to Elsie's, and sat and chatted for a while. Eddie had brought her a drawing from nursery school, a boy and a woman with green grass and a blue sky. It looked pretty good to me. Elsie was ecstatic. She had already cleared off a space on the front of her refrigerator and put it there with magnets.

"That's my picture," Eddie said.

"It's wonderful, Eddie. Is that you?"

"Uh-huh. And that's Elsie."

"It looks just like her. That's a terrific picture." In a way it did look like Elsie. She has a very round face, and that's what he had drawn. In fact, there wasn't much else to the figures besides the faces, but that was OK with me and obviously with Elsie as well.

We went home and I stopped thinking about Darby Maxwell and got to work on dinner. Eddie did a lot of talking and I listened carefully. Some girl in his class had smeared paint on someone and then there was a big fight. It wasn't clear whether the paint smearing was an accident or had been done intentionally, but the whole incident had made a great impression on my son. I guess the boy who got painted was pretty mad, and I imagined the teacher must have had quite a row on her hands. Although I kept it to myself, I was rather pleased that a girl had been the instigator. There are times when I really believe strongly in equal opportunity.

"That's quite a piece of information," Jack said that evening after I'd told him about the sneakers. "She never told anyone?"

"No one official." I sketched out how she had felt during that period.

"I understand and I sympathize, but I hate loose ends. And that's one hell of a loose end."

"What do you think the police would have done if they'd known?"

"They could've canvassed the area, found out if someone was missing a pair of sneakers. Maybe someone invited him in."

"And didn't call the police," I said.

"Or worse."

I didn't want to think about worse. "Well, I knew you'd be interested. When she told me, it took my breath away."

"You know, there's always the possibility that the young man Darby was visiting gave him the sneakers. They may have been up in the kid's room before they went walking."

"It's so long ago, it hardly pays to ask. And suppose that's what happened. It doesn't change anything."

"But suppose that's not what happened. It's a very tantalizing situation."

That would have been the end of it, except that the next time I visited my friend across the street, Melanie Gross, I told her what had happened. Twelve years ago she wasn't even married, and she bought the house in Oakwood only six or seven years ago, before I moved into Aunt Meg's house. Still, she's always interested in the little stories I dig up, so I told her about Darby and the sneakers and my aunt.

"There have to be a lot of explanations for those sneakers," she said. "Did I tell you about the time Noah went to school wearing one shoe and one sneaker?"

I laughed out loud. "No, you didn't."

"I don't know what he was thinking, but that's what happened. They sent him to the nurse, of course. Poor nurse gets all the problems no one else can solve. She called and I dashed over with a second sneaker. I nearly died of embarrassment."

"I can see why. But you can't dress them forever."

"Hardly."

"Mel, do you know a woman in town named Laura Filmore?"

"Laura? Sure. Marvelous woman. She volunteers at the school a few days a week, helps out with kids who read below grade level. She's patient and kind and works very hard. You couldn't pay someone to do a better job. Why do you ask?"

I went through it all again, the carton, the papers, my aunt's kindness.

"I'll introduce you to her if you're ever over at the school. You'll like her."

That was the Monday after I had visited Betty Linton. The next afternoon, I went to the school around closing, taking Eddie with me. I told him he would go to this school in a couple of years, and he stood beside me watching the children pour out of the building, run to hug their mothers, and laugh with their friends. They must have looked big and forbidding to him, because he stayed very close to me, holding my hand. Suddenly he caught sight of Sari Gross and he relaxed his grip and pointed.

"Look," he said. "There's Sari. Does she go to this school?"

"Yes, she does."

"It's a good school," he said. "But I like my school better."

"Right now I think your school is a better place for you. Look; there's Mel."

We walked over and Mel gave Eddie her usual enthusiastic greeting. "Chris, this is Laura Filmore. Laura, Chris Bennett Brooks."

"Glad to meet you." She held out a hand and shook mine. "Mel tells me you're Margaret Wirth's niece."

"Mommy," Eddie said, "I want to go home with Sari."

"Oh, no," I started.

"No trouble," Mel said. "Come on, Eddie. Let's find Noah and we'll all go home."

That left me with Laura Filmore. I waved good-bye to my departing son, who couldn't have cared less at that moment, and walked along with Mrs. Filmore. "Yes, I'm Meg's niece and I live in the house she owned."

"I felt so bad when she died. She was a fine person, a real asset to our community."

"Thank you. I learned about you just recently." I told my story one more time as she listened attentively.

"That was a very terrible time and Meg was very helpful through all of it, my husband's disappearance and then his death. But she was that kind of person. I'm glad to see you're raising a family here in town."

"I've lived here since I was released from my vows, and my husband moved in when we married."

"Oh, yes, the niece who was a nun. I remember now. You used to come and visit."

"Once a month so I could see my cousin at Greenwillow."

"You are certainly bringing back a lot of memories." She stopped walking, rested her briefcase on the back of a black car. We had been going through the teachers' parking lot. "I'm really very glad to meet you. We should get together for lunch one day when I'm not at school. I have to run now if I'm going to get something for dinner."

"Would you like to join us tomorrow night?" I asked, surprising myself as the invitation came out. One thing I am not skilled at is dinner parties.

"What a nice idea." She smiled. "Yes, I'll be glad to."

"We live on—"

"Oh, I know where you live. I've visited that house many times."

"Great," I said, although I could feel palpitations. "If you come at seven, I'll have Eddie off to bed."

She laughed. "Seven is fine."

Jack was stunned. "Just like that you invited someone to dinner?"

"Just like that is exactly how it happened. I think I said the words before my brain knew what my mouth was doing. I've had a lot of second thoughts, but the truth is, I'm glad I did it. I'll be teaching tomorrow morning, so I can pick up one of those wonderful pies the food service students make."

"Make it two pies," my hungry husband said. "You know, to give our guest a choice."

"OK, two." I elbowed his ribs to let him know he wasn't putting anything over on me. "But I'm glad I invited her. She's alone and I'm sure she'll appreciate a nice hot meal."

"As long as it isn't convent stew."

"It won't be convent stew. I think I'll make my stir-fry with lots of good mushrooms and those great snow peas." That's been my fail-safe meal for as long as I've known how to make it, courtesy of Mel, for whom everything works in the kitchen.

"Sounds good. How 'bout a nice red wine?"

"That's your department. I'll polish up some of Aunt Meg's good crystal so we can drink it the way it was meant to be drunk."

"Sounds like a feast. Hope the lady appreciates it."

Laura Filmore arrived precisely at seven, just a few minutes after I had gotten Eddie off to bed. She gave me some flowers and I'm sure she could tell how much I appreciated them. We all sat down in the family room and Jack offered drinks. I declined—I needed my full intellectual powers and energy to get this dinner to come off right—but Laura Filmore accepted a Scotch on the rocks with a little water. I was glad I'd gotten some bottled water for the occasion.

The first thing she mentioned was how the house had changed. "It was such a small house when I visited," she said, looking around the spacious family room. "Adding this wonderful room changes everything."

Jack, who had initiated the addition, told her about our master bedroom suite right above it, and she commented approvingly.

"I'm glad you're so happy here. Meg would be pleased. She loved this house; she loved living in Oakwood. She would be so happy to know that her home has been improved and another family is growing up here."

She had a lot of questions for both of us, about how we met and when we moved here and what we thought of some of the projects in town.

Jack had offered to do the cooking, but I felt this was my show and I had a mental schedule of when everything had to be done so we didn't sit and get hungry all night. I excused myself at the precise moment and got things going, and I must say, although it was a simple dinner, I didn't embarrass myself. Everything was ready on time and tasted good. Jack poured wine into Aunt Meg's sparkling crystal glasses and I was happy once again that I had the opportunity to use them.

Finally, as the evening went on and we ate our two pies with coffee, Laura told us a little about what had happened to her husband. "I thought fifty was a great opportunity to celebrate," she said. "I couldn't make it a surprise—it was too big and there were too many people involved—although I did have some surprise guests that made my husband very happy. You know, when I sent the invitations, I called it the happy birthday party. That's how I felt about it. He was truly at the prime of his life. On that night he had—or so I optimistically thought—half again as many years to live, and probably more. How could I possibly have known that he had only a few days to live? And why?"

Why, of course, was the question.

Jack leaned slightly toward her. "I'm sure you dug deep trying to find a reason somewhere in his life."

"As deep as I could go."

"And everyone you know has asked you if you had even the slightest suspicion that something was troubling him."

"Everyone from his mother to his casual acquaintances. There were no secrets, either bad or good. His finances were in perfect order. He hadn't made any promises he hadn't kept. No mysterious calls ever came either to his office or to our phone at home. It is the deepest sadness of my life that something was troubling him and I knew nothing about it."

"I was very sorry to hear about it," I said. "Reading the notes I discovered and the holy cards made me feel as though it were all very fresh."

"Your aunt was wonderful to me, not that I was surprised. She was that kind of person and she'd had her share of troubles."

"There was no note?" Jack asked.

"There was nothing. There was my husband's body and a gun."

"Was it his gun?"

"I don't know. It wasn't registered to him. I think he may have owned one, but we never talked about it. But they couldn't trace this one to anyone else."

"It had a serial number?"

"Oh, yes."

"Interesting," Jack said.

"There was just one strange thing about his body, and I've never found an answer to that, either."

We both looked at her expectantly.

"He was wearing casual clothes, slacks and a golf shirt, the same clothes he was wearing when he left the house. But I'm sure the sneakers weren't his."

6

I stared at her, then turned to Jack. This couldn't be. This was too much of a coincidence. I wanted to say something but couldn't find the words.

"Is something wrong?" Laura asked, looking from me to Jack and back again.

"Did you ever know a young man named Darby Maxwell?" I asked finally.

"Can't say that I did."

"He was a resident at Greenwillow at the time your husband died."

"The home for retarded adults that moved into Oakwood a few years ago?"

"Yes."

"What I know about them is what I heard from Meg. Her son lived there. I assume he still does."

"He does, yes. He's my cousin. Darby Maxwell was his friend, and he died within a few days of your husband."

"What does one thing have to do with the other?"

"That's what we're trying to figure out," Jack said. He explained how I had discovered that Aunt Meg had known both families and had attended both funerals a dozen years ago, that Darby had apparently been lost in the woods and died of exposure. "Chris just met Darby's mother recently, and she said when Darby was found he was wearing someone else's sneakers."

"That can't have anything to do with my husband," Laura said. "There can't be any connection. Greenwillow wasn't even here in town at that time, and Larry wasn't involved with it."

"What color were the sneakers he was found in?" I asked.

"White. Larry always wore black. And they weren't even his size. They were too small for him. I don't know how he squeezed his feet into them."

"Darby was found with black sneakers," I said. "The ones he had on when he got lost were white."

We were all quiet for a few moments. I could almost hear our thoughts, feel our tension.

"I can't believe there's a connection," Laura said finally.

Then Jack said, "Think about it, Laura. Your husband's death may not have been a suicide."

She had walked into our house a very self-possessed woman, sure of herself, confident, a woman who knew her way around. Now she sat with her fingers touching her lips, her face pale, a tremor moving her head. "I can't believe this," she said. "I would love to find out that Larry didn't kill himself, but what does this mean? That someone may have murdered him? That's almost harder to believe."

"Both men died within a couple of days of each other. Chris has the dates. There are newspaper clippings her aunt kept. Did your husband know anyone in Connecticut?"

"Well, yes. We have friends there. Why do you ask?"

"Darby died in Connecticut," I said. "How many miles did your husband put on his car between leaving you after the birthday party and being found?"

"I don't really know. He always put the trip odometer back to zero when he bought gas and he had filled the tank two days before he disappeared, but I don't know how much he drove in those two days."

"But it gives us a maximum."

"It was two hundred and some miles. He probably drove less than two hundred while he was away."

"Maybe we should start from the beginning," Jack said.

"I can't. This is too upsetting. I haven't really accepted what you've told me. I want to go home and think about it. Maybe we can talk tomorrow, Chris," Without waiting for an answer, she stood and walked to where she had laid her handbag a couple of hours ago when we were all beginning what we thought would be a friendly dinner party. "Thank you both. It was a lovely evening, at least until a few minutes ago." She smiled. "I'm so happy to have met you and to have seen what you've done with the house. Chris, I will call you tomorrow; I promise. We'll talk. I just can't do it now."

"Did you tell the police about the sneakers?" Jack asked.

"It's so long ago I don't remember, and I wasn't thinking straight. I was just trying to get through each unhappy day."

"Do you have the sneakers?"

She looked thoughtful. "I may. I'm not sure. I will look."

We walked her to the front door and then out to her car. She gave each of us a hug and thanked us again. Then she got in the car and drove away.

While we were clearing up and getting the dishes taken care of, I thought of Betty Linton. It wasn't ten yet and I told Jack I would give her a call.

A man answered and called Betty to the phone. I told her who it was.

"Chris, how nice to hear from you."

"Betty, I know it's late to be calling, but something unusual has just happened and I wanted to ask you a question about Darby."

"Of course."

"You told me he was wearing someone else's sneakers."

"They were black and his were white."

"Did you check the size?"

"I don't remember doing that."

"Do you still have them?"

"They're put away, yes."

"Would you know if they were Darby's size?"

"Yes. I bought clothes for him. I had all his sizes written down. I remember his shoe size was ten D."

"If you have a chance, could you check those sneakers he was wearing?"

"I'll do it right now. If I don't call you back tonight, you'll hear from me tomorrow."

"Good thinking," Jack said when I put down the phone. "This has to be the craziest thing I've ever heard."

We tidied up the kitchen and went upstairs. Eddie was sleeping soundly. I fixed the blanket and leaned over to kiss him, then went to our room and started undressing. As I was putting on my robe, the phone rang.

"Chris? . . . This is Betty. I found the sneakers. They're size eleven and a half. They're much bigger than Darby's. I don't know how I didn't notice."

"It was a very upsetting time. Thanks for checking."

She asked what it was all about and I told her briefly.

"You mean there may have been foul play?"

"It looks that way."

"How can that be?"

"I don't know, but I mean to find out."

"I'll do whatever I can to help."

I woke up on Thursday morning feeling very excited. Facts and possibilities were buzzing in my head. I hoped I would hear from Laura Filmore because I wanted to know everything she could tell me about the birthday party and the events that had followed. We had our breakfast and Jack drove off to New York, where he has been working at One Police Plaza since he finished law school a couple of years ago.

It was a raw day and Eddie and I dressed warmly. He had a new red flannel shirt that he wanted to wear, and I thought this was a good day for it. When he had it on, he went to the mirror in my bedroom to look at himself.

"It looks great," I said.

"I like it. Does Daddy have a red shirt?"

"I'm not sure. Maybe we should give him one for Christmas so you can both dress up the same."

"OK," he said, smiling.

"Just don't tell him, OK?"

"I promise."

I wasn't sure he would keep the promise. He had spilled the beans on a Father's Day present I had wanted to keep secret, but that was several months ago. Maybe, I thought, he had matured since then.

We were making his bed when the phone rang.

"Chris, this is Laura Filmore."

"Good morning. I hope we didn't give you a sleepless night."

"It took me a while to fall asleep, I admit that, but I slept well. I found the sneakers Larry was wearing. As I said, they're white and they look fairly new. The size is ten and I think there's a *D* after the number."

"That's the size Darby Maxwell wore," I said.

"We need to talk about this, Chris. I have to be at school this afternoon. Is there any chance you're free to come over this morning?"

"Will you mind if I bring my son?"

"Not at all. I have a roomful of toys. He'll have a good time playing while we talk."

"Half an hour?" I asked.

"Please."

The house was brick with stone accents, a fairly grand structure in a section of Oakwood that had large, expensive houses on large pieces of property. Some had pools in the backyards; some had tennis courts. All were landscaped magnificently. Laura saw us coming and had the door open when we walked up the path. She took us to a large room with a playpen, a rocking horse, and about a million toys and games, the room, she said, where her grandchildren played. Eddie was delighted. When he was settled, she and I retired to the room next door.

"I feel very confused," she began. "I don't know what's going on and I can't see how my husband's death can have any connection to the death of the young man you described. Why didn't anyone see it when it happened?"

"Because the bodies were found in two different states with two separate police forces and the causes of death seemed clear-cut. Mrs. Linton, the mother of Darby Maxwell, said her son's clothes were returned to her sometime after the burial. Darby walked away from his mother and friends and disappeared for a long time, a week or so, I think. When his body was found, a determination was made that he had died of exposure. The nights had been cold; he looked as though he'd been out-of-doors. He was found in Connecticut, not far from where he was lost."

"And my husband was found here in Oakwood. I see now why you asked how many miles were on his car. Tell me again what connected the deaths of these two people in your mind?"

"My Aunt Meg attended the funerals of both. Your husband's was here in town. Darby's was nearby, because his mother had lived north of here at one time and Darby lived at Greenwillow."

"And somehow the sneakers were exchanged. Is it possible that it happened during the autopsies?"

"I can't see how. Darby died in Connecticut. The autopsy was up there."

"And Larry died here. I see your point. Neither police department had any reason to question the other. I don't even know if Larry went to Connecticut during the days he was missing."

"But he could have, according to the mileage."

"This is frightening and distressing. What do you think we should do about it?"

"I think to start I'd like to hear your story right now, with dates and times and everything you can remember. Then I'd like to get you together with Betty Linton and have you talk this over, see if there's any connection between your family and hers."

"You mean if there's anyone we know in common."

"Yes. Or perhaps your husband and her husband worked in the same place years ago, or something else that I just can't think of at this moment."

"Then let me get started." She took a breath. "I planned the party. As I said last night, it was Larry's fiftieth birthday and I wanted to get friends and relatives and other people in his life together to celebrate. I have an invitation here, if you care to see it."

I took it from her outstretched hand. It was the same embossed card with brightly colored candles forming a border on all four sides that I had found among my aunt's papers. I noticed that the address was that of the church in town that we go to, and a reply was requested. A note at the bottom asked that no gifts be given, but contributions could be made to some named charities.

"I designed the cocktail napkins with the same border," Laura said, "and the words 'A Happy Birthday Party for Larry Filmore' in the center. I had thought of having it in a hotel or some elegant place, but in the end, I felt we were residents of Oakwood, our lives were here, and this was where we should celebrate."

"Mrs. Linton felt that way about Darby's funeral. She lived in Connecticut when he died, but she wanted the residents of Greenwillow to be able to attend. She had it in the church they used to go to."

"So Meg, who knew both of them, went to both funerals."

"As did Celia Yaeger."

"Celia, of course. She would know about Darby because she knew Meg's son."

"That's right. Go on with your story."

"It was a wonderful party. We had about four hundred people, including some who traveled from Europe and Asia to join us. There was a band and a lot of dancing. The music ended at one, and Larry and I hung around talking to friends for another twenty or thirty minutes, although many had gone by then. Our children had been driven home earlier. We had to carry some things out to the car, I remember, a case or two of liquor that hadn't been used and a bunch of gifts from people who just couldn't come to a birthday party without one. Then we drove home."

"Did you empty the things in the car?"

She thought for a moment. "No, I think we didn't. We were really very tired by then. It had been an exhausting day. Larry opened the trunk and took out some of the presents, but he didn't feel like hoisting the cartons of bottles. So we left them there."

"Were they there when his body was found?"

"I think they were. You can understand they weren't the first thing on my mind."

"Of course. And then what?"

"We went in, we set the security alarm as we always did, and I think we just went upstairs. No, maybe Larry stopped at the refrigerator for a glass of something cold."

"Check the answering machine?" I asked.

"I doubt it. Everyone I knew in the world had been at that party. Anyway, in the kitchen we would have heard it beeping if there'd been a message."

"So you went upstairs."

"We didn't go to sleep right away. As tired as we were, we were very excited. We had seen people we hadn't seen in years. A friend had flown in from Tokyo for the occasion and there were other people who came from great distances. We got ready for bed and sat in our little sitting room for a while, just talking, rehashing. I was so happy, Chris. It had been such a wonderful evening. It wasn't the champagne that had made me high; it was the happy memories."

"And your husband?"

"Exactly the same. Larry acted as though it had been a surprise. He hadn't known who was on the guest list, except for the obvious people, and he talked about how some old friends looked, what they were doing. He told me . . ." She faltered for the first time and I sat and waited. "He told me how much he loved me." Tears spilled down her cheeks. "But there was nothing of a farewell in what he said. He was looking forward. He said maybe we would return the favor and take a trip to Tokyo to visit our friends there. I think he was just as happy and excited as I was." She looked away and I could imagine that she was remembering the last happy moments of their life together.

"I'm sorry this is so painful," I said. "Perhaps—"

"No, we have to do this. Let's see. It must have been at least two-thirty when we went to bed, maybe even as late as three. I had no alarms set. We agreed to sleep in. We turned the lights off and that was it. The night of the happy birthday party was over."

What she had told me sounded very ordinary, just what I would expect after a party like the one she had described.

It was the next step that I thought would be telling. "Do you think you can go on?" I asked.

She nodded. "I don't really know what time it was, but it wasn't light yet, so it might have been four or five and it couldn't have been much after six. The nights were getting longer, and I know it was dark. The phone rang. The sound worked itself into whatever I was dreaming, so I didn't react to the first ring, and obviously Larry didn't, either. But when I realized someone was calling in the middle of the night, I awoke in fear. Larry's mother was not young and she had come to the party. She had left early and gone home, but what if she had become ill? I heard Larry answer the phone, but he didn't say much, just syllables and grunts. When he hung up, he said something like 'a problem at the plant.' He had to go.

"I remember saying, 'Let someone else go, honey. You need your sleep.' But he was already out of bed and getting dressed. He said I should go to sleep and he would see me in the morning."

"Did your husband own a gun, Laura?"

She took her time answering. "He did. It was licensed and all that, perfectly legal. He had owned it for many years, but as far as I know, he had never used it."

"Do you know where he kept it?"

"No. I wasn't happy when he brought it home and I said I didn't want anything to do with it."

"Is it possible he took it with him?"

"It's possible."

"You never found it anywhere in the house?"

"I never looked for it."

"But it would have turned up if you looked through his things."

"I went through his whole chest of drawers after he died, a while after, and it wasn't there. I wasn't looking for it, you understand. But I would have found it."

"Was there a place in the house he might have hidden it? I've heard that people put valuables in the freezer sometimes."

"There was no gun in the freezer; I would know. If he really hid it, it could still be hidden."

"Did he go directly from the bedroom to the car?"

"I think so, but I can't be sure. Once he was out of the bedroom, I couldn't really tell you where he went. Most of the floors and all the stairs are carpeted, so there's no noise. He went downstairs and a few minutes later I heard the car pull out of the driveway."

I knew what she was thinking, that after that she never saw him again. As she had spoken, I had almost seen what happened, the man getting out of bed, pulling on convenient clothes, sticking his feet into favorite sneakers, saying good-bye, and going down to the car. And how many times after that had she asked herself why she didn't press him on what was happening? Even now, even a dozen years later, the agony of remembering was all over her face.

"That was it," she said. "I never saw him again."

7

We took a break at that point. Laura offered me coffee, but I preferred a glass of juice, as did Eddie, who was having a great time on the rocking horse. The area of the room he was playing in no longer looked as neat as when we had come in, but I decided to leave the cleanup till we were ready to go or I'd have to do it twice.

After our break, Laura and I went back to our respective places. "When did you sense something was wrong?" I asked.

"I got up about ten, later than I usually did. Larry wasn't there. I went downstairs, called him, then looked in the garage. His car was gone. So I called the plant and talked to the weekend watchman. He seemed confused when I asked him if my husband was there. He must have thought I had gotten the day wrong. As far as he knew, nothing had gone amiss during the night, he certainly hadn't called our house, and Larry had never been there. I felt confused myself, and when I sat down to think it all out I got frightened. I called the local police there and asked if anything had happened near the plant overnight and they said no. I told them what had happened and they said to wait awhile; he would surely come home. Probably I had misunderstood."

"It's pretty standard for the police to tell you to wait," I said. "Most people do come home."

"But Larry didn't. I let the Oakwood Police know what

had happened and they put out an alarm for Larry's car. I called people, but no one had seen him since the party. I don't know what else to tell you, Chris. That's how it happened. No one that I know saw Larry alive after he left our house."

"Can you tell me about when you found him?"

"He left the house in the early hours of Sunday. You can imagine I was a wreck after that. There were no sightings, nothing. I kept in touch with the police, but they came up with nothing. My sister-in-law came to stay with me, and my children were home. It seemed so strange to have a house full of visitors when all the joy in my heart was gone. Four days after Larry left, in the early hours of Thursday, I thought I heard a sound in my sleep, a bang, but I turned over and ignored it. In the morning, I went downstairs for breakfast and opened the door to the garage as I had been doing each morning since he left and there was his car. I had one moment of absolute joy, as though there had been a reprieve, as though everything might be right again. I was wearing a robe over my nightgown and I dashed over to his car to see if he was there. The garage door behind the car was open, which surprised me, as we never left it open. I got to the car, calling his name, and then I saw what had happened."

"How terrible," I said.

"I know I screamed. I could see he was dead. There was blood everywhere. I think I stood there for a moment, covering my eyes, crying, screaming. Then I ran inside. My sister-in-law was in the kitchen, on her way out to find me. I screamed, 'He's dead! He's dead!' over and over again. My sister-in-law had her arm around me and she reached for the phone and called the police."

"Did it look to you like suicide, Laura?"

She nodded. "He was shot in the right temple. He was right-handed. They said there were powder burns on his skin. His fingerprints were on the gun. What more could you want?"

"I think you told me it wasn't his gun. Is that right?"

"It wasn't licensed to him. The police checked. There was something strange about the ownership. I think it had been stolen some years before. I asked them not to check further. I suddenly had a crazy thought that maybe Larry had traded in his licensed gun for this one. I don't know how he came to have it, whether he owned it or found it or what. I just didn't want anything besmirching his name. The Oakwood Police knew he owned a gun, but that wasn't it."

"So they never found out who owned it?"

"Not after it was stolen. Larry had shot himself and I didn't care whose gun he had used. He was gone and I didn't know why. People offered explanations, but they were halfhearted. They wanted to make me feel better, but nothing could make me feel better. Not then and not now."

"How do you feel about talking to Betty Linton?"

"I think I have to. Now that you've uncovered this strange connection of the sneakers, I think we have to talk."

"I'll set it up. It's almost noon and I know you have to be in school. Take it easy for a bit, Laura. This has been a terrible morning for you."

"If we can make sense out of what happened, I will always be grateful to you."

"Let's just take it one step at a time."

I called Betty Linton, who knew nothing of the sneaker mix-up, and filled her in. She was as startled and uncomprehending as Laura Filmore had been, and as interested in meeting Laura as Laura was in getting together with her. I arranged for Laura and me to drive up to Connecticut the next day. Eddie would be at nursery school in the morning, and Elsie would take care of him in the afternoon. I told Betty to think carefully about the people she had known twelve years and more ago, as we would try to compare lists to look for an overlap. I knew that was a difficult assignment. After so many years, it's hard to remember the names of the neighbors and coworkers, club members, classmates, and other casual acquaintances, but I had nothing else to go on and somehow Darby Maxwell and Lawrence Filmore had crossed paths during the time both were missing. I didn't think they knew each other, but some person or some odd situation must have brought them together. I started thinking about degrees of separation. Who or what had been the unlikely link between these two people?

Laura and I talked all the way up to Connecticut on Friday morning. Jack had given me some ideas of questions to ask, and Laura had come prepared with a couple of file folders of what might be pertinent information.

When we reached the Lintons' house, Laura exclaimed at how lovely it was. It changed her mood from the dark of the trip to almost light. She parked her car and Betty came outside and greeted us.

Inside, we sat at the dining room table so the women could spread out their papers. There was plenty of time before lunch, and we got started right away.

"We can flip a coin," I said. "I think we should go back twelve years and each of you should talk about addresses, businesses, vacations, friends, and other people you knew. Let's see if we can find a match somewhere."

Laura began. I had my notebook open and I jotted down what I thought might be important as she spoke. She had lived in Oakwood for most of her married life and had met her husband while she was working in New York when she was in her twenties and he was working in his father's business. They had owned two houses, a small one in the early days of their marriage and the current one, which they bought when their second child was born.

Betty Linton's life was quite different. She and her first husband had married after she graduated from college almost forty years ago. They lived in an apartment in New York for a little while, then bought the house north of Oakwood. When Darby was born, the marriage began to crumble, although they stayed together for many years. There were visits to doctors and other experts, but the doctors Laura had known were not among them. There were therapies and special schools and finally, when Darby was old enough, residence at Greenwillow. Eventually, there was a divorce. Today Charles Maxwell was remarried and living in California.

Betty had met Brad Linton soon after her separation. A widower, he had children in college and a demanding job. They had bought the house in Connecticut just before they married, each of them selling an old house and starting anew by pooling their resources.

It got to be twelve-thirty and we had found no intersection of the two women's lives. They looked drained, as though they had spent time working out-of-doors instead of sitting in this comfortable room going through papers and talking.

"Let's have lunch," Betty said, pushing away from the table. "We're not making any headway here. Maybe we need our energy refreshed."

We all got up and went into the kitchen, each of us doing part of the chore of setting the table. Betty had salads in the refrigerator, so there was little work to do besides getting the coffee going. As though by mutual consent, we talked about other things while we ate, Laura admiring the antiques, Betty asking about my cousin Gene.

When we were done and the table had been cleared, I made a suggestion. "If it wouldn't be too hard on you, Betty, I wonder if you would take us to the house where Darby disappeared."

"I can do that. What do you expect to find?"

"I'd like Laura to see where it is in case the area rings a bell. And then, if you're up to it, I'd like to walk through the woods and see where we come out."

She took a moment before answering. "Let me call my friend. She still lives there."

"That's a good idea," Laura said while Betty was telephoning. "What you're thinking is that somehow my husband and Betty's son crossed paths during the days that my husband was gone."

"I can't see any other way that they could have exchanged sneakers."

"Any other explanation would involve a lot of moving people or things around. If Larry drove up this way to see someone, for whatever reason, and somehow stumbled onto Darby—"

"Or stumbled onto a person who was with Darby."

"Yes, I see. Darby could have asked someone for help or knocked on someone's door."

"My friend said it's fine to come over," Betty said, coming out of the kitchen. "She has a dentist appointment and won't be there by the time we get there, but she's given us carte blanche to walk around the property and into the woods."

"Then let's go," I said.

It was a twenty-minute ride and we followed Betty's car. The whole area was very beautiful, houses of many ages set picturesquely far from the road, up little hills, almost hidden by old trees and shrubs. Betty pulled into a long drive and parked at the side of an old house that was beautifully cared for. We got out and walked on a flagstone path around to the back.

"You can see they have a lovely piece of property," Betty said, leading us away from the house. "They actually own a few feet of land beyond where the trees start. We were sitting over there." She pointed to where garden furniture still stood. "We had all had lunch and the boys got up and started to walk. My friend was showing me some pictures of a vacation they had taken, so my attention wasn't on Darby."

We reached the woods and kept walking, moving into the dark forest as though through Alice's looking glass. It was a different world. The trees were now bare and the floor of the forest was almost soft from the many layers of leaves. We kept to a path, but after a while it dwindled into nothing.

"Did they bring dogs to help find him?" I asked.

"Yes, but somewhere around here they lost the scent. They said it seemed that he had gone around in circles. Anyway, they continued onward, the way we're walking."

"Do you know your way?" Laura asked, her voice tight.

"I do now. I walked it so many times after Darby disappeared, I think I could find my way in the dark."

"I can see how you could get lost here very easily. *I'm* not even sure how to get back."

"Don't worry. I know the way."

But Laura's observation was the same as mine. Without the sure guidance of Betty Linton, I would already have lost my bearings. A tree I had sighted as a landmark now seemed in the wrong place. I took a moment to pivot, looking in every direction for light from a clearing, but I found none. I thought of the lost boy, the young man with the mind and fears of a boy, and I felt his anxiety as though it were my own. Had he called for his friend or his mother?

I wondered. At what point was he too far from them to be heard? When did he become desperate?

We continued on and I began to have my own fears, that maybe Betty had not been here for so long that she could lose her way as her son had, had perhaps already lost it and wasn't aware. I was third in line as we walked, my eyes peering forward for the inevitable light, or the light that I hoped was inevitable.

And then I saw it. I felt relief and wondered if Laura did, too.

"We're coming out," she said ahead of me, and I could hear the joy in her voice. She had been even more frightened than I.

"Yes!" Betty called, turning back to us. "It's just up here."

A few minutes later we entered a meadow. My eyes hurt from the bright light. I stopped and looked around, hoping to find a house nearby that might have been a place where Darby knocked on a door for help, but I saw nothing except more trees beyond the grass.

"Where's the nearest house?" I asked when we were together in the sunlight.

"It's still some distance from here. There's a small lake or pond over that way." She pointed left. "Through another patch of trees. People swim there in the summer, not many, but it was too cool that day for anyone to go into the water."

"How do they find their way?" I asked.

"There's a path from there that eventually gets to a road. I don't know if Darby saw it. If he had found it and stayed on it, he'd be alive today."

I turned to Laura. "Does anything here look familiar?"

"Far from it. I'm sure I've never been here in my life."

"Did your husband ever talk about going to Connecticut? An old swimming hole? Friends from his childhood?"

She shook her head. "Never. Absolutely never."

"You want to go any farther?" Betty asked.

I looked at my watch and saw that Laura was doing the same. "Not today. But I may come back, if you don't mind, and go as far as you can take me. I'm especially interested in seeing the houses that Darby might have stumbled on."

"We can do that whenever you like." Betty turned back to the woods we had left and started walking.

We went single file again and I remained last. On the return walk we were mostly silent except when Laura tripped over an exposed root and nearly fell. I dashed up to help, but she had grabbed onto a branch that steadied her.

"You all right?"

"Yes." She was out of breath and looked scared. "I should have worn better shoes."

"It's my fault. I should have mentioned what I had in mind."

"You certainly work hard at this, Chris. Maybe you'll do what no one else has done."

I patted her shoulder. "Let's wait and see what happens. We're a long way from finding out the truth."

We started walking again. Betty had stopped to wait for us. Now she took up the lead and we followed. After about five minutes, Betty stopped and looked around.

"Is anything wrong?" Laura called.

"No, I'm just trying to get my bearings."

"Do you mean you're lost?" Again Laura's voice was tight with fear.

"I think I got turned around a little. Stay where you are. I want to check something." She took off.

Laura looked at me. "She's lost, isn't she?"

"Let's just wait," I said calmly, although I didn't feel entirely calm.

"She hasn't been here for years. We should have gotten a guide or put markers along the way."

I had no idea myself where we were. I looked up through trees that were losing their last leaves. When poor Darby had been here, it had been earlier in the season and there had been more leaves on the trees, making it darker. I looked around, trying to see or hear Betty, but she was gone. Beside me, Laura Filmore was almost shaking.

Then a voice came from somewhere ahead and to the right of us. "Yoo-hoo. Can you hear me?"

"We're over here!" I called back.

"I found the path. Can you follow my voice?"

"We're coming."

"Keep talking. I'm standing still. Can you see me yet?"

"Not yet, but we're moving toward you."

Then I saw something red through the trees. "There she is, Laura. She's waving her red silk scarf."

"Yes, I see it. Thank God."

"Here we are, Betty!" I called.

"Follow me. We'll be back at the house in a few minutes."

Five minutes later we came out of the woods behind her friend's house, all of us having learned a lesson. The forest had its own rules and no one's survival was guaranteed. Betty had lost her way and some of her confidence, but we were safe and happy to be back.

We discussed another meeting and then we separated and all drove home.

8

"She was lost, wasn't she?" Laura said after we got on the main road and were heading home.

"I think she was, but not badly. She found her way pretty quickly."

"I wouldn't want to do that again."

"I understand."

"What are you planning to do, Chris? I'm sure neither I nor my husband had any connection to that part of Connecticut, and you could see from our discussion that our lives never intersected. I don't see how you're going to put Larry together with Betty's son."

"I want to put your husband and Betty's son together with an unknown third party, although it's possible your husband stopped at the side of the road and picked up Darby."

"If that had happened, Larry would have seen to it that Darby was returned to his mother or at least to the police."

"Which is why I think the other possibility is more likely."

"But why the switch of sneakers? I just can't see how that happened."

I had given it a lot of thought over the last days. "I think your husband was sending a message. He must have realized that there was a good chance that he would die or that Darby would die and, at least in Darby's case, it might look like a natural death, the effect of weather and lack of food. He probably was able to convince Darby to switch sneakers, hoping that when his mother saw him she would see they weren't his and she would know someone had a hand in his death. The same goes for your husband's body if and when it was found."

"So you don't think the switching was an accident?"

"No. It must have been very uncomfortable for your husband to wear shoes that were too small. I think whatever situation they were in, whether they were in the hands of some maniac or someone that your husband had dealings with, he sensed that they might not survive."

"Why didn't he write a note and stick it in his pocket?"

"Because the person who was holding them was too clever for that. He may have confiscated pens and pencils. Were there any in your husband's personal effects?"

"No," she said after a moment, "but he left in a hurry. He had his wallet, which had his driver's license, but that was all."

"And Darby probably didn't have anything with him, either. He was wearing casual clothes. I'll check with Betty anyway, but that's what I'm thinking right now."

"How will you proceed?"

"Two directions," I said. "I want to find all the houses that Darby may have come across. I want to talk to any people who remember what happened twelve years ago. And on the other hand, I want to find out all I can about your husband's past. Do you have a problem with that?"

She changed lanes before she answered, checking mirrors carefully. "No, I don't. Larry was an honest man. He paid his taxes; he treated his employees well. I saw many of them weeping at his funeral. He had many business associates, a lot of whom came to the birthday party. He had good relations with them. I will help you check him out in any way I can."

"Thank you. You told me yesterday you asked the police not to investigate the ownership of the gun that killed him."

"I was feeling a little crazy at the time, Chris. I don't know how he got it or where he got it, but he obviously got it somehow. Maybe a business acquaintance gave it to him for protection."

Or he got it illegally himself, I thought.

"Something you said a few minutes ago," she said. "About pens and pencils. They were on his dresser, Chris. I found them there in the morning after he left. But nothing else was there. And now I think about it, when the medical examiner sent back his personal effects, there was no small change, well, maybe a few cents, a nickel and some pennies. And he always had a pocketful of change."

"He may have spent it," I said.

"He could have, but if he was in captivity, as you suggest, he may have been forced to give it to his captor."

"Right."

"I remember being surprised when I opened the bag with his wallet, but then I thought maybe someone in the medical examiner's office had taken it for himself."

"That's always possible, but the police inventory everything they remove."

She drove without speaking. I knew she was thinking of possibilities she had not considered before. I was glad we were on this trip together with no one else around and nothing to disturb us.

"And the wallet," she said. "There was only one bill in it, a ten or twenty. Larry always carried a lot of money with him. It worried me, but he said you never knew when it would come in handy. I would bet he left the house with at least two hundred dollars and a pocketful of change."

"And there was no money in the bedroom?"

"None at all. His good pen was there; I remember that. I gave it to my son sometime later. And a ballpoint he always carried in case he had to sign something with duplicate copies." Her voice had turned urgent and eager. She was remembering things that had been mere facts at one time but that now had become meaningful. "But no money. And you know what? I remember hearing him gather his coins and drop them in his pocket before he left. You know how you hear something and later it comes back to you and makes sense? That's why it struck me as strange that there were almost no coins and bills left. I know he took it all with him."

"You never made inquiries?"

She let her breath out. "When I saw the sneakers and knew they weren't Larry's, I called up. I think I may have told you. The man I spoke to took offense. Acted as though I was accusing him of theft. So when it occurred to me, somewhat later, that the money was wrong, I didn't want to call up again. Sneakers are one thing; money is much more serious."

"This is very interesting, Laura. What you're suggesting is that his captor may have taken most of his money—not all because it would be too obvious—before he was killed. He left just enough that it wouldn't look as though he'd been robbed, at least not to the police."

"You think Larry didn't kill himself," she said.

"I don't know. Can you think of anything that might make him want to?"

Again she took time to answer, as though she was really trying to think of something so terrible that her husband would choose to end his life. "What would make a happy man kill himself?" she asked.

"The discovery of some old misdeed, some personal failing, some accident that may have looked like an intentional crime."

Her face had grown very somber. She stared straight ahead, guiding the car through traffic. "Not Larry," she said. "I knew Larry most of his life. He told me everything. I was his closest confidante. There were never any times when he didn't come home or disappeared for long periods of time. We kept in touch, even before the era of cell phones. If he was going to be late, he called me."

"You said he owned a gun."

"Yes, but he never shot anyone."

"But you don't know where it is."

She shook her head. "I wish I did."

"Will you look for it?"

"I will. I'll search the house. I know it isn't in the safe-deposit box because I've emptied that. I've never really looked for it. I will now."

"Good."

"This has been a very productive drive."

"It has. Let's keep up the good work."

Eddie was glad to see me and I equally glad to spend some time with him. As usual, he had some wonderful craft he had made in nursery school, a kite painted with bright colors, and I admired it and he told me how he had made it.

Finally he said, "I'm hungry."

"What would you like?"

"A chocolate chip cookie."

"Did Elsie make them for you?"

"Yes." He smiled at me. He probably knew Elsie had given me a doggie bag with at least half of what she had baked.

"Let's see if I have any," I said. I opened the drawer where I kept pretzels and cookies, my junk food drawer, and looked inside, knowing they were not there.

"I don't want those cookies. I want Elsie's."

"I wonder if I have any."

"You have them. I know."

I gave him a squeeze and a kiss. "You're right. I just remembered where they are." I went to the cabinet and took them out.

We sat at the table and munched on a couple. Elsie is a dream. If I didn't have her, my whole life would be different, and nowhere near as complete. The chocolate bits melted in my mouth. I was glad Eddie had brought up the subject.

"That's an interesting theory," Jack said when we were alone in the evening. "That Filmore was sending a message."

"The only other possibility is that the killer made them switch to make Filmore uncomfortable. But if he was smart enough to make a suicide look real, he wouldn't have wanted anyone finding the body—or bodies—to notice something wrong with the clothing."

"You're right. And if Filmore had no other way to get the word out, that would have done it. I'm sure he never imagined his death would be made to look like a suicide, but he might have thought his body would be dumped somewhere or even hidden, possibly never to be found. But if Darby's body was found, his family would know the sneakers were wrong."

"What Filmore didn't count on was that the bodies would be found in two different states. That really changed things."

"It did. And also that the clothing wasn't returned to the families till later. So where are you going from here?"

"I'm putting together a bunch of questions to ask Betty. And I want to investigate Lawrence Filmore's past."

"I'll see what I can find on Monday. Does his wife know you're doing this?"

"Yes, and she gave me her permission. She doesn't think I'll find anything."

"She may not know." Jack got up, got a sheet of paper, and folded it twice, writing below a folded edge. He asked for whatever information I had, address, age, birth date.

"I'm going to go to the plant he owned," I said. "Laura gave me the address and some names before she dropped me off. They make upscale leather items, like belts and handbags and wallets. Her father-in-law started the business after the Second World War, and Larry went to work there out of college. So that was his life."

"And all the organizations he worked for."

"It's hard to believe anyone in a charitable organization would murder a donor."

"You don't know what their relationships were. You keep referring to the killer as 'he.' Maybe he fell for a woman at the Find a Cure for Cancer charity."

I smiled. "Here comes the deep, dark side of Jack Brooks."

"Murder's pretty deep and dark. You think everyone who works for the good of mankind is good? You want me to cite chapter and verse?"

"Please don't. It's bad enough when I hear about it on the news."

"Got some news myself. I signed up for a course to prep for the lieutenant's exam."

"That's great." He had been studying by himself for several months and this was the next step. "When will it start?"

"After the first of the year. It means nights again, honey. Can you take it?"

"If you can, I can." The first few years of our marriage Jack had gone to law school at night, then studied for the bar. Having him home on a regular basis was a continuing gift, but I knew he wanted to advance and this was the way up.

"Glad to hear it. Got any more of Elsie's cookies?"

Two of a kind, I thought.

9

The next morning I called Betty Linton. Jack and I had continued our conversation the previous evening, and he had suggested some questions for me to ask.

"I hope I didn't scare Laura," Betty said. "She seemed very tense. I wasn't really lost. I just wanted to come out behind my friend's house, not a house down the road. Some of the neighbors are a little sensitive about trespassers."

"She's fine. It was a very instructive hike. We could both see how easy it would be to get turned around or walk in circles."

"And Darby never went walking alone. Even now, I shudder when I think about how he must have felt."

"Betty, I want to ask you about what happened during the time he was missing. Did you publicize his disappearance?"

"Oh, yes. I was on local radio several times. I taped a plea for people to look for him. And I was on television with a picture of him."

"Anything else?"

"A bunch of us put up flyers on trees and poles with a picture and my phone number."

"Did you offer a reward?"

"Ah." She paused. "No, we didn't. There was a lot of discussion about it. I would have paid the person who found him everything I own; I'm sure you understand that.

But there was something wrong with offering a reward, as though he were a piece of property, not a person. The experts we talked to thought it was better not to."

I agreed with her decision and the reasons that led to it. "Did anyone call during the time he was gone?"

"Several people. No one said they had him in their living room. Mostly they thought they'd seen him in one place or another. I let the police know whenever I got a call like that."

"Did you take their names and numbers?"

"Yes, I did. But nothing ever panned out, as you know."

"Did anyone ever call asking for a ransom?"

"You mean as though he had been kidnapped?"

"Yes."

"No. And we didn't think that had happened. There was one call, though." Her voice drifted off.

"What was it?"

"It was probably just someone looking to pick up some easy cash. He asked if there was a reward."

"What did you say?"

"I asked if he knew where Darby was. He said he didn't, but he would really look hard if there was something in it for him."

"What did you do?"

"The police had a trap on my line and they traced the call to a pay phone in town. No one was there when they got there. There was a flyer on a pole right near the phone, so I assumed the man had seen it, put a quarter in the phone, and called me up. It was annoying, but I didn't really think much of it. He sounded very rough, if you know what I mean."

"Did the police follow up on it?" I asked.

"There wasn't much they could do. Phone booths are full of fingerprints. In fact, I think they said when they got there a woman was using the phone. I don't think it was anything serious, Chris."

I was making notes as we spoke. I've learned not to overlook what other people think of as unimportant details, not that I thought this was necessarily meaningful. And I was well aware that whoever made the call was lost to me.

"You're probably right," I said.

"What were you thinking of?"

"Just that perhaps Darby strayed into the home of someone who thought he might use the situation for personal benefit, try to extort money for Darby's return."

"Nothing like that happened."

"I'd like to go to the houses that Darby might have found, if you know where they are."

"I have a map that shows a lot of details, including houses in the area. After twelve years, I'm sure many of those people are gone."

"Even so."

"Then let's do it. You've made me feel that the explanations I accepted may have been wrong. If there's a truth I don't know, I'd like to find out what it is."

We made an appointment for next week and she promised to find the list of houses and locate them on a map.

I was aware from listening to the news over the years and from talking to Jack about interesting cases that in kidnappings there were often calls from pranksters and opportunists. The fact that the phone booth the man called from was right next to a pole with a flyer probably indicated opportunism more than anything else, although you never could tell. It was certainly heartwarming to know that people believed they had sighted Darby—and maybe one or more of them had—and had taken the time to call. If there had been a ransom demand, the police would have followed up on it, no question about that.

With arrangements made for the Darby side of the case, I called Laura Filmore and asked whether I could talk to people at the plant her husband had owned. She had already checked and found that the night watchman who had been on duty the night her husband disappeared was still working there and still working nights. I didn't look forward much to talking to someone in the hours after midnight, as I am the opposite of a night owl, but I thought I could get there by seven in the morning if he would be there tomorrow. She called me back fifteen minutes later and said Charlie Calhoun would be there overnight and if I got there at eight, when he went off duty, we could have a cup of coffee and talk in the cafeteria. I promised to be there.

For all the years I lived at St. Stephen's, I got up at five in the morning. Getting up at six-thirty was a piece of cake, and I could be back home in time for a real breakfast and mass.

"One more thing," I said, winding up the call. "Now that we are pretty sure your husband was in Connecticut during his disappearance, can you go back over your guest list and let me know what people at the party came in from Connecticut?"

There was no answer.

"Laura?"

"I can't do that."

"What do you mean?"

"I knew you would ask. I told you very truthfully yesterday that I didn't know anyone in the part of Connecticut we visited, and none of the people Betty knew matched the ones I have known, but I can't give you any names."

"Then there were guests from Connecticut."

"There were and they weren't involved. I would stake my life on it."

"How close were they to where we walked in the woods?"

"They lived within the range of mileage on Larry's car," she said evasively. "I didn't mention them because I can't let you talk to them."

"Laura, I don't think you can decide in advance—"

"I have decided," she interrupted. "That's it. It's final."

"I hope you change your mind," I said. "If you do, you can call me."

"I won't. That's the end of it."

It was the end of our conversation. I had thought she had been completely forthcoming in Betty Linton's house yesterday, but obviously she had kept this to herself. I was annoyed, but there wasn't much I could do. Even if I could find people who had been at the party, they were unlikely to recall, after so many years, out of four hundred people the name of one person or two who might have driven down from Connecticut. I would have to let it lie.

In the meantime, there was the delicate matter of finding out whether there were secrets in Lawrence Filmore's past. Since Jack has a good relationship with the Oakwood Police Department, he went over there in the afternoon to see if he could wheedle information out of them. He was gone longer than I thought he would be, and Eddie and I had come home from our walk when he finally pulled into the driveway.

"Took some doing," he said, patting Eddie on the back.

"Where did you go?" Eddie asked.

"I had to talk to a policeman."

"I wanna talk to a policeman."

"They're very busy, Eddie. Maybe another time."

"Learn anything?" I asked.

"He had a pretty clean record. Coupla traffic violations, nothing serious. The file on the suicide is closed: no crime, no case. No one offered me a peek and I don't want to upset anybody by being pushy. That's the quickest way to wear out your welcome in this business.

"Someone at their house was once rushed to the hospital during a party. One of the older cops remembered it. They thought it was a heart attack, but it turned out not to be serious. I don't think there's anything there."

"I'll ask Laura," I said, making a note in my book. It was surely something she would remember.

"I'll get on the computer on Monday and see what I can find out. I'll check his wife out while I'm at it."

"Laura?" I said with surprise.

"Why not? Doesn't hurt to cover all bases. So you're getting up at the crack of dawn tomorrow?"

"A little after the crack. And I'll be back by the time you two lazy guys are getting up."

I told him later about Laura's admission.

"I can understand it," he said. "Suppose I had to say whether my mother or sister had been somewhere that might make her a suspect in a crime. I'd sure as hell rather not connect her, even if I was absolutely sure she'd done nothing."

"If there's one thing I've learned in looking into all these cases in the last few years, it's that you don't know anyone except yourself. It's true I trust you completely, but I've seen trustworthy people lie and evade the truth so many times that I can't dismiss the possibility that the Filmores' friends in Connecticut are in some way connected to his death."

"You're right to be skeptical, Chris, but maybe Laura's friends are people going back to early in her life, or maybe even a sister or brother. Think of how they would feel if they knew Laura had given their names as possible suspects."

I understood, but it hampered my investigation. "Doesn't

matter," I said. "She's not giving up the names. I'll have to work around it and hope they're not the ones."

On Sunday morning my old habits kicked in and I awoke five minutes before the alarm went off. I crept out of bed, thinking how strange it was to see Jack lying there fast asleep. Typically, he's an early riser like me, and on weekends, if he gets up before me, he lets me sleep.

I dressed quietly and went out to the car. It was so still out, I could hear every rustle of the leaves as I walked back to the garage. Laura had given me driving instructions, in fact the exact route her husband always took from Oakwood, and I followed it to see what he had always seen and to time it.

I arrived at the plant before eight and parked in the visitors' area, although the lot was almost empty. They closed on weekends, and I assumed the few cars were those of security and maintenance staff. Inside, I found a stocky middle-aged man in a uniform sitting inside a room with a bank of TV monitors, a round desk with enough lights to decorate a Christmas tree, and a black walkie-talkie station. It all looked pretty high-tech to me. I knocked on the door and he looked up and waved me in.

"You must be Mrs. Brooks," he said.

"I am. And you must be Charlie Calhoun."

"Right you are. Why don't you take a seat in one of the comfortable chairs outside? My replacement's in the building and I'll be out as soon as he signs in."

"Fine."

I went out to the lobby and sat in a maroon chair that was truly comfortable. I had hardly taken my coat off when a young man in the same security uniform Charlie Calhoun was wearing came into the lobby.

"You waiting for someone?" he asked.

"Mr. Calhoun."

"He'll be right out." He went inside the office and Charlie Calhoun emerged a moment later, carrying two large cups of coffee.

"This way, ma'am."

"I'm Chris," I said. "Let me take one of those coffees."

We walked down a long hall and into an empty cafeteria. He turned the lights on and we sat at a table for four near a window. Outside were woods. It seemed a lovely place to eat a meal.

"I'm Charlie," he said, offering his hand. "Mrs. Filmore said you think the boss didn't kill himself."

"There's a good chance he didn't. I don't know if I can prove it, but I think it's worth a try."

"Well, if it hadn't happened the way it did, I wouldn't've believed it, either. He wasn't the suicide type."

"I'd like to assure you that anything you tell me will not get back to Mrs. Filmore."

He grinned at me. "What? You think I'm going to rat on the boss? No way. There's nothin' to rat about. He was as good a boss as you could find. Once when I got some real bad news in the middle of the night, he came over and sat here so I could go home. They don't make 'em like that anymore."

I agreed. "But there may have been people who didn't see eye to eye with him."

"There always is. He got in a shoutin' match once with a young guy who was new and was takin' advantage. That's a long time ago and the little creep didn't have the guts to hurt anyone anyway."

"You have a name?" I asked.

"Not at this late date. I prob'ly wouldn't recognize it if I saw it."

"Mrs. Filmore said you were on duty the night Mr. Filmore disappeared."

"I'm on every Saturday night, unless I'm sick or on vacation. I swing out, you know, off on Sunday and Monday, so I was here."

"Mr. Filmore told her, after he got off the phone in the middle of the night, that there was trouble at the plant."

"I been over this with the police a thousand times. There wasn't no trouble, nobody ever called except my wife, and I never saw him."

"Could someone else have called to tell him there was trouble that night?"

"Don't see how. I don't think there was another soul in the building. They was all at the party. You know about the party?"

"Mrs. Filmore told me about it. Is there a reason why you didn't go?"

"I'm not much of a party man. You gotta get dressed up—that was a fancy shindig, you know?—and they needed someone here like always. Mr. Filmore, he said he'd get another guard, you know, from an agency, but hey, they don't know the place like a regular. I said just save me a piece of cake; I'll stick with the job."

"I guess you never got the cake," I said.

"You know what? I did. He made an arrangement with the caterer and they delivered a little box with a big piece of cake in it. He was that kind of man. He never forgot a promise."

"What kinds of problems might come up during the night?" I asked.

"Oh, a lot of things. Round that time we had problems with the furnace. After Mr. Filmore died, they just replaced the whole thing. Pretty expensive, but it hadda be done. Sometimes the power would go off in a storm. We also have a lot of chemicals and leather, so the fire alarm system has to be watched for smoke and water leaks. Once a vagrant came in and I couldn't get rid of him. Don't ask me how he found this place. It's off the beaten track, to say the least."

I had thought so myself as I drove to it. "Did Mrs. Filmore take over the business after her husband died?" She had told me she had.

"Yeah, for a while. But it wasn't right for her. She started comin' in days like her husband did, but after a coupla months she hired a plant manager and some other people to run the business. She still owns it, and she comes in once in a while, specially around the holidays, but she don't run the place anymore."

That squared with what she had told me. "I'm sure it's a very hard job," I said.

"You gotta know a lot and she didn't. Everybody helped, but she could see it wasn't working out. She did what was right for the company."

"And I guess you're happy working here."

"It's a great job. I'll retire in a few years with a nice pension. Then I'll have to learn how to stay up when it's light out." He grinned again.

There didn't seem to be much else I could ask. We had both finished our coffee and I was sure he wanted to get home. "Bottom line," I said, "you didn't call the Filmores that night."

"No, ma'am. Didn't call and didn't have a reason to. It was a quiet night. I didn't hear till Sunday afternoon when the police came that he was missing, and I couldn't believe it."

"Sometimes you remember things," I said. "Here's my phone number if something comes to you. Anything at all. I really think there's a good chance someone killed Mr. Filmore and I'd like to find out who."

"I'll think about it," he said, gathering the cups and napkins from the table.

We went out to the parking lot together, shook hands, and walked to our separate cars.

I hadn't expected to get anything useful from Charlie Calhoun, so I wasn't disappointed. Nor did I think he was holding back. He had seemed quite up-front and I believed that his affection for "the boss" was genuine.

I got home to find Jack and Eddie putting together a Sunday breakfast with bacon and eggs. The coffee smelled a lot better than what I had drunk half an hour earlier.

"Where did you go, Mommy?" Eddie asked as I took my coat off.

"I had to talk to someone very early."

"A policeman?"

"No, sweetheart, not the police." Obviously he remembered where Jack had gone yesterday afternoon.

We all pitched in and had a good breakfast and went to mass. In the afternoon, we picked up Gene and took a drive that ended with a sundae at one of our favorite places. I enjoyed the feeling of relaxation with my family, knowing that after today I was going to be very busy looking into the case.

When I got into bed many hours later, I picked up a mystery by Agatha Christie, one that I had never read. It put me in the mood of my students, and I liked that.

10

My day began early on Monday, as soon as Eddie was off to school. I drove up to Betty's house and got there at midmorning.

"She's a nice woman," Betty said when we were inside.

"Yes, she is. And she's lived with this terrible uncertainty for a dozen years. She's never been able to figure out why her husband would take his life, especially after one of the happiest occasions he had ever experienced."

"Let me ask you something, Chris. If we establish that Laura's husband's death is somehow connected to Darby, does that mean that Darby may have been murdered, too?"

"I think someone may have contributed to his death, not that someone shot him or anything like that, but that in some way this person prevented Darby from being found."

"I guess that means I have some unhappy times ahead of me, thinking about how he was treated."

"Does that change how you feel about pursuing this?"

"It's too late to stop now that we've started. Come into the dining room. I've got stuff spread out all over the table."

Most of the things on the table were maps, interesting maps. One was an aerial view with the house Darby had started out from, the woods behind it, clearings, ponds, more woods, and a number of houses he could have reached, although they were fairly far from his starting point, a mile or more. And on the perimeter were roads. If only you knew where you were going, you could reach a road. It made the tragedy seem that much worse when you could see rescue so close at hand.

"You know," I said, looking at that map, "if Darby took a turn here or here," I pointed to two places perhaps half a mile from a road, "he could have ended up on a busy highway."

"What are you thinking?"

"That it's possible, now that I see the whole layout, that he did get to a road and Larry Filmore might have picked him up."

"Why was Larry Filmore there?"

"When we know that, we'll know why he left home in the middle of the night and what the great secret in his life was. All I'm suggesting is that he may actually have been a Good Samaritan. He's driving to meet whoever called him at home, he sees Darby at the side of the road, realizes he needs help and he's not a threat, stops, and picks him up."

"Darby knew his name and my address. Why didn't he return him to us?"

"Because he was in a hurry. Whoever called him threatened him in some way. If he had stopped to find where Darby lived, he wouldn't have arrived at his destination on time and something terrible would have happened. That's my theory."

"So the Good Samaritan delivered my son into the hands of a killer."

"Possibly. Remember, that's only one explanation of the facts. It's equally plausible that Darby knocked on a door himself, one of these houses here."

"There was a lot of publicity, Chris. The police drove along roads with loudspeakers."

"Betty, it's very unlikely that Larry Filmore found Darby in the woods, sat down with him and exchanged sneakers, and let him go. It defies explanation."

"You're right. Their paths crossed either at someone's house or, as you suggested, in Larry Filmore's car. Why did Larry Filmore kill himself?"

"I don't know. Maybe someone made a terrible threat against his family and he knew the threat would evaporate if he was no longer living. And maybe someone very clever killed him and made it look like suicide."

"And Laura has no idea what this is about?"

"Not at all. He left the house and was found a few days later in his car in his own garage, dead of a single bullet to the side of his head. The gun was next to him."

We stood there looking down at the dining room table with the maps spread over its entire surface. Then Betty said, "Let's get started."

We folded the maps and went out to her car. This time I had come prepared for the woods. I had bought myself a small compass. With that and the maps, I had more faith in my ability to find my way back to a starting point.

This time we didn't start from the friend's home. Instead, Betty drove us to a rural area at the eastern end of the map, where three houses stood along a rustic road, a few hundred feet apart from each other. The first two were brick and could have been fifteen or twenty years old, although I'm no expert. The third one, farthest down the road, appeared to be an old farmhouse.

"These two," Betty said as she turned into the first driveway, "belonged to a mother and daughter. The mother was in her sixties twelve years ago and the daughter was married with two children. The name here is Warren."

We got out of the car and went up to the front door. A chime played a short tune when Betty pushed the button, and the door was opened almost immediately by a white-haired woman wearing dark brown wool pants, a yellow shirt, and a camel-colored sweater over it.

"I know you," she said, looking at Betty as though trying to pull a name out of the past.

"Betty Linton. My son, Darby Maxwell, was lost in the woods twelve years ago."

"Oh, yes, the poor child. Come in; come in. It's cold out there."

We went inside to a very warm living room with a woodstove in the fireplace. The heat that radiated from it was very strong, and I could imagine it warmed the whole downstairs. We made introductions and sat down.

"I remember you now," Mrs. Warren said. "My husband joined the search party back then. Your son died, didn't he?"

"Yes. Thank you for helping."

"That's when I met you; I remember now. You came by afterward to thank us."

"Yes. A lot of people were very helpful. I'm eternally grateful."

"You don't find many people anymore who say thank you. I'm sorry it turned out the way it did."

"Mrs. Warren, some new information has been found. We think Darby may have spent some time in a house before he died."

"It wasn't here. We would have turned him in."

"I know that. But maybe you've heard something over the years."

She shook her head. "It's pretty lonely out here. My daughter who lives next door didn't say anything and our neighbor down the road—I don't know if they were there when it happened. They're away a lot."

"Mrs. Warren," I said, "do you know people around here who own guns?"

"Hunting guns? Lots of folks have 'em. My husband used to do some hunting. When he died last year, I got rid of the gun."

"I was thinking more of handguns."

"That's harder to know about. Probably the police know. They've got to be licensed."

"Back when Darby got lost, were the people around here longtime residents?"

"All three of these houses had the same people in them. The neighbors farther down, the Gallaghers, they bought that house about twenty years ago. Now there's other houses—no, they're newer. They weren't here then. But if you go up this road to the end and turn right, there's other houses there."

Betty was shaking her head. "He would have come to this road first."

"You're right. Poor thing. Such a sad way to die."

"Did you ever know anyone named Filmore?" I asked. "Lawrence Filmore and his wife, Laura."

She shook her head. "I knew a Laura, but it's not Filmore. Talk to my daughter, girls. She's home now and she's much more outgoing than I am. She's active in the garden club and the church and she does some volunteer work at the school. She knows lots of people. But she doesn't have any guns."

"Thank you," I said.

We got up and left.

"Sure, come right in." Mrs. Warren's daughter, Michelle Franklin, was effusive in welcoming us. "Make yourselves comfortable. I'll fix us some coffee."

Before we could decline, she was off to the kitchen, banging things around, calling to us to sit wherever we wanted. Five minutes later, she was carrying in coffee cake that looked wonderful and then the rest of her offering.

"How's Mom?" she asked as she poured coffee into flowered mugs.

"Oh, you mean your mom?" I said.

She laughed. "I haven't called her yet today."

"She's fine. That's some wood-burning stove she's got over there."

"Aren't they wonderful? Her heating bill is almost nothing. That little stove just pours its heat all over the house. We've got it fixed so it goes up to her bedroom through a vent in the living room ceiling. There we are. Sugar? Cream? This is great cake. My friend baked it yesterday and I just happened to visit and came away with a nice chunk."

It took a while to steer her to the subject, but when we did she remembered the search for Darby and a lot of details that impressed Betty.

"Our kids were young then," she said. "My father joined the search party right away. They had a skirmisher line— you know how they walk in a line touching fingers? I don't think he came home till almost morning."

"Do you know where they started from?"

"Where the boy was last seen, southwest of here. My husband couldn't join the search because he was out of town when it happened, but I went into the woods back there," she pointed toward the rear of the house, "and did some looking myself. I never saw any trace of him."

"Do you know who found him?" I asked.

"That was old Mr. Dailey. He's gone now. He was out with a whole lot of men and he sighted the boy first. At least that's what they said." She turned to Betty. "This must be very painful for you."

"I need to find the truth," she said. "Don't worry about me. Just keep talking."

"What can I tell you?"

"We think Darby may have stopped at a house in the days before he was found."

"I don't think so," Michelle said. "Everyone knew he was missing. There were flyers all over town, on the school bulletin board; they talked about it at church. I even saw you on television," she said to Betty. "Why would anyone take him in and then not call the police?"

"We aren't sure," I said. "I thought maybe someone you know might have let something slip over the years."

She shook her head.

"Were there any empty houses or barns in the area at that time?"

"There are lots of empty barns and some empty houses. I'm sure the police checked them all out. They really worked very hard to find him."

"What about the people next door?"

She wrinkled her nose. "I can't remember exactly, but I know they usually go away around Labor Day for a few weeks. That happened in September, didn't it?"

Betty nodded.

"They were probably away. They're a couple with grown children now. He does some computer work and he's been working out of the house for a long time, from before when it became the thing to do. She does some work at the hospital, in the accounting department, I think."

"Are you friends?"

"We've known each other a long time and we get together, but we're not close friends."

"And you think they weren't home when Darby disappeared." I made a note in my book.

"It's hard to tell. They often drive up the road that way." She pointed toward the house next door. "We usually go the other way. So if they don't pass my house, I don't know if they're home or not. I don't really see their house through the trees. And frankly, there's no way they would take in a boy like your son and then just let him go. They're good people."

I asked if she knew anyone named Filmore and she said she didn't. "Wasn't there a president with that name?"

"With two *l*s. This one has only one."

"Sorry."

We left a little after that. The couple next up the road were Dave and Frannie Gallagher and we drove over to see if they had anything to contribute. The door was opened by a tall man in black corduroy pants, a gray knit shirt, and a black sweater over it. He called his wife, who came into the living room and greeted us.

"I don't have much time," she said. "I'm due at work."

"Just a few questions, Mrs. Gallagher." I explained quickly what our mission was and asked if she remembered what had happened.

"We were away," her husband said. "When we came back, we heard about it, but it was all over."

"Do you leave your house locked when you're gone?" I asked.

"Oh, yes," his wife said. "Always. We even have lights that go on and off. Dave jokes that it's to keep the squirrels happy, but I like to think it's a kind of security."

"Does anyone ever look into your house when you're away?" Betty asked.

"Only if we're gone a month or more, and that doesn't happen very often."

"Have you ever known a Lawrence Filmore? Larry Filmore and his wife, Laura?" I asked.

They looked at each other. "Never heard the name," Dave said.

"Me, neither." Frannie looked at her watch. "I'm sorry, but I've gotta run. I'm on afternoons this week."

We were still wearing our coats. Frannie put hers on,

grabbed her purse, gave her husband a quick kiss, and the three of us went outside.

"Nice to meet you!" she called, taking off for her car, which was in the driveway next to Betty's. "Hope you find what you're looking for."

We went into town and had lunch, taking our maps and notes into the coffee shop with us.

"It's very discouraging," Betty said. "Not that I had any reason to think we'd find something new."

"Don't be discouraged. We're just starting. We may stumble on information and not be aware that it's relevant right away. But my impression of the three families we've talked to is that they're not suspects. They didn't cringe when I mentioned the name Filmore. Somewhere along the way, someone may."

"You're right. I'll have to watch their faces when you ask the question. But from what I've seen, we can scratch these three houses from the list. One helped in the search, one doesn't seem likely, and the third was out of town."

"Maybe," I said.

"What?"

"Maybe they were out of town."

"What an awful business this is," Betty said sadly. "You have to keep thinking that people may be lying to you."

"The trick is to figure out which one."

Betty opened a map and folded it. "Want to pick the next place we look?"

"Let's just take whatever is closest to where we are now. And before we do that, do you remember where that phone booth was that the man who called you used?"

"It's across the street. We can walk by it on the way to the car. How do you plan to find out whether the Gallaghers were really out of town during that time period?"

"I'm not sure," I said. "If they didn't have children in

the schools, it's likely to be difficult. It's so long ago at this point that I wouldn't expect the post office to have a record of holding their mail or of the newspaper a suspension of delivery. I'll think about it."

"They were probably gone," Betty said. "Michelle Franklin is the one who first suggested it. If it's something they do every year—"

"You're right. It would stand to reason that they did it that year, too."

"OK. I'm done with my coffee. Are we ready to go?"

"Absolutely."

We crossed the street and went down the block to where a phone box stood. Beside it was a pole that carried electric wires.

"The flyer was just about here," Betty said, pointing to a spot about eye-high. "I seem to recall they were about six by nine inches with a picture of Darby taking up the top half. The word *lost* was in heavy print, I think above the picture."

"So he read it as he walked down the street and then just stepped over to the phone."

"Or he could have seen it on that pole across the street and come over here to the phone." She pointed to another pole, almost exactly opposite where we stood.

"OK," I said. "It's reasonable to think that's what happened."

"Ready to move on?"

"Ready."

11

We drove to some houses to the north of where Darby had disappeared. The first one had been sold, bought, sold, and bought again in the intervening years. The current owner had no idea who the owner had been twelve years ago and didn't even know for certain where the most recent former owner now lived. Down the road was a larger house with no one home. I could sense Betty's disappointment. But the third house yielded a talkative woman who remembered the incident and had been at home the whole time.

"Oh, yes," Mrs. Delia Farragut said. "It was all over the news. My son, who lives a mile or so from here, was in the search party. It was your son it happened to?" She looked at Betty.

"Yes, it was."

"You poor dear. I am so sorry. What is it you ladies are trying to find out all these years later?"

I explained and she nodded, leaned back in her rocking chair, and said, "I see. But I don't have a clue who would do such a thing. And why? You think maybe he was kidnapped?"

"Not kidnapped. We think maybe someone took advantage of a situation."

"I see, yes. Took advantage. People do that, don't they? Did you pay someone money?"

"No," Betty said. "We're just trying to find out what happened."

"The people two houses down that way, did you know them?" I asked.

"The Criders? I knew them. Moved out a long time ago."

"How long?"

"That house was up for sale for almost a year. They thought it was worth a whole lot more than it was and they wouldn't come down. When they did, they sold it pretty quick and moved out even quicker."

I knew we could check the date of sale at the town hall, but I asked, "Do you remember when they moved?"

"They sold it just before Labor Day to a family that had two children that they wanted to put in the schools here. They didn't quite make it for the start of the school year, but they closed sometime in September, maybe the last day, maybe a week before."

"What year was that?"

She looked a little puzzled. "The year we were talking about, whatever it was, the year the boy disappeared."

"You're sure of that?" I said.

"Sure I'm sure. I remember the night they came over to say they had a bona fide offer on the house. They were so happy, you'd think they'd won the lottery. They started packing the next day."

"Do you know where they went?"

"Somewhere warm. They'd had another house for a long while, Florida maybe. The Carolinas." She looked thoughtful. "Could even have been Arizona. I wrote it down, sent them a Christmas card for a couple of years, then didn't bother when they stopped. You know how it is? They tell you to come and visit and then they don't really invite you."

"Could you find the address?" I asked.

"If you pushed me, I guess I could." She looked at both of us, gave us a grin, and got up. She was in the kitchen for several minutes, and when she came back she had a piece of paper with her. "Found it in the old, falling-apart address book that I've never had the heart to throw away. You never know when you'll need it, like now, right?"

"Thanks so much for looking," Betty said.

"It's Florida after all, West Palm Beach. Does that ring a bell?"

"I've heard of it," I said.

"You gonna call them?"

"I may. What can you tell me about the people right next door?"

"The Pasternaks? Nice people, good neighbors."

"How long have they lived there?"

"Must be twenty years now."

"Were they here when Darby was missing?"

"Must have been if they've lived there twenty years."

"They're not home," I explained. "That's why I'm asking."

"They're working. They both work."

She didn't seem to want to say any more, so I asked about the next house along the road.

"Down that way? That's the Wilsons. I don't know them too well. They built that house maybe ten years ago."

"So you don't think they were here when Darby was lost?"

She thought about it. "Maybe they were building the house then, but I don't think so. I think they moved in later. Cleared a whole lot of trees to build that house." She seemed sad at the thought. "I can give you their number if you'd like. Harry and Diane." She gave me the number from memory. "She might be home now, but he won't. You can give 'em a try."

"Mrs. Farragut, did you ever know anyone named Filmore? Larry and Laura Filmore?"

"Don't think so. You think they live around here?"

"No, I was just wondering."

"Sorry."

Betty and I got up and we both thanked her. She told us
to come back soon, but I took it the way she took the invitation to Florida, a pleasant way to say good-bye.

We sat in the car for a few minutes while I made some
notes and clipped the phone numbers to my page.

"Did we learn anything?" Betty asked.

"I'll call Florida tonight and see if the Criders are still
at this number. There's something a little strange about
their moving out right after Darby died, but life is full of
coincidences."

"Especially if they'd had the house on the market for
such a long time and they had another one ready to go to."

"Right." I looked at the next name on the page. "Are you
ready to try the Wilsons?"

"I guess we could, but it sounds as though they didn't
live there twelve years ago."

"Then we won't spend much time."

Betty backed out of the driveway and went up the road
to the next house. It was quite a beautiful house, very
modern, with beautiful wood and lots of glass. I could
imagine it had taken a while to build it and to clear the lot
as well. There were still plenty of trees around, and I
thought they must have tried hard to preserve as many as
possible.

The woman who answered the door was dressed in a
black pantsuit and heels, and I had the feeling she was getting ready to go out. We talked to her for only a couple of
minutes, standing in her foyer, which was lighted with a
skylight two stories above us. They had bought the lot
eleven years ago and moved in nine years ago and she

didn't know anything about anyone who had been lost in the woods.

When we got back in the car I felt we'd done a day's work. I had a child to go home to and a call to make to Florida. Betty drove us back to her house and we went inside.

"Where do we go from here?" she asked. We were in the dining room and she laid the maps on the table.

"There are more houses, more people to talk to. If you'd rather not join me, just give me the maps and I'll do it myself."

"I don't know," she said. "I think I'm finding this very depressing. I don't like to see you out there all by yourself, Chris."

"Don't worry about me. I've been doing this for several years and I'm always alone."

"Are you sure?"

"Positive."

"Then take the maps. Call me if you need information on anyone at all. There's a list of names and addresses in there somewhere. If I can add anything, I'd be glad to."

I picked up the pile, glad I would be able to look at it all at my own pace.

"You'll call, won't you?" Betty said.

"Of course."

She leaned over and kissed my cheek. "Thank you for doing this."

"Let's hope we learn something."

Jack brought home only a small amount of information about the Filmores. "There's nothing of importance on either of them," he said in the evening. "They're not wanted anywhere. They have no arrest or prison records. It looks pretty dull, the way your record or mine would look."

"That dull?" I asked.

"Yeah, that dull. But remember, computers only go back so far. This guy died a dozen years ago and computers don't go back a lot more than that. So if there's something from way back, it'd take a lot more work to find it."

"I wasn't really expecting anything."

"But I found out about the gun that was used in the Filmore suicide."

"Laura said it was stolen or something."

"That's true." He leafed through some pages of notes and pulled one out. "The gun was a Smith and Wesson six-shot made in 1968. Twenty-five hundred of these were bought for use by the NYPD."

"It was a cop's gun?" I said.

"Looks like it. He lost it in Harlem, Two-Six Precinct, in a bad snowstorm in '69."

"He lost his gun?"

"That's what the Oakwood Police have. He reported it lost, got a complaint for 'failure to safeguard a weapon,' a trip to the department trial room, and a five-day rip. Sorry, I mean a five-day suspension of pay, a fine." He looked at me. "You're not supposed to lose your gun."

I smiled. "Gotcha."

"The gun was recovered in the Filmore car and it made the department and the ATF happy. Nobody likes loose ends, especially when they involve guns."

"So anyone could have it."

"And probably did. Filmore could've picked it up somewhere. Whoever he went to Connecticut to meet that night could've had it. They gave me the name of the guy that lost it." He handed me a sheet of paper. "And I looked him up. Believe it or not, he's still on the job after all these years. He's a one-twenty-four man, you know, clerical duty, property clerk vouchers, gofer, down in a Brooklyn precinct."

"Jack, that's great."

"He's probably old and fat and slow. He works eight-to-four tours, Monday through Friday."

"Which makes it easy for me to drop in on him." I looked at the name Jack had written down. "P.O. George Reilly."

"Thirty years ago you still had a lot of young Irish cops."

"I'll try to get into the city this week. But the gun was lost for quite some time, so it could have passed through a lot of hands."

"And maybe it did. If it was Filmore's, I'd like to know who he got it from."

"If Larry Filmore had a registered gun, it's hard to believe he'd have an unregistered one, too."

"Stranger things have happened."

When Jack says something like that, he's not talking hypothetically. It's because he's been involved in cases where such things have happened. But nothing that I knew gave me a clue to whether the suicide gun was Filmore's or someone else's.

I called Laura after we'd had our coffee and went through the list of names of families we had visited, or tried to visit, during the day.

"Alice Warren?" she said. "I knew a Barbara Warren once. She'd be about my age."

"Too young. Her daughter's name is Michelle Franklin."

"No."

"Dave and Frannie Gallagher?"

"Doesn't sound familiar."

"Crider," I said. I read from the piece of paper. "Joe and Bea Crider."

"No."

"Ever know a Pasternak?"

"Never."

"Delia Farragut?"

"Sorry." She sounded sad.

"Those are the ones we covered today. They live in an area where Betty's son might have knocked on a door."

"I wish I could help you."

"I'll check back when I have some more."

When I got off the phone, I called the number in Florida I had gotten from Delia Farragut. A woman answered.

"Mrs. Crider?" I asked.

"Yes. Who is this?"

"My name is Chris Bennett. I'm looking into an incident that happened in the part of Connecticut you lived in some years ago."

"We haven't lived there for a long time."

"I know that. Do you remember when a retarded young man was lost in the woods?"

"Yes, I do. It was just before we moved."

"That's the one. What do you remember about that?"

"Well, I know he got lost in the woods and I remember they found him dead somewhere, but I don't recall where. My husband thought about joining the search, but we had just agreed to sell the house and we had so much packing to do, he just didn't have the time. Why are you asking?"

"We think the young man's death may not have been accidental. I just wondered if you might have come across him or if you knew anyone who did."

"I certainly didn't." She sounded a bit indignant. "And I don't know anyone who did. If I knew, I'd have told them to call the police."

I knew I was antagonizing her. "What about the people right next door to you?" I asked.

"The Pasternaks?"

"Yes. I rang their bell today, but they weren't home."

"I don't know anything about them. You'll have to talk to them yourself."

She was the second person who didn't want to talk about them. "Do they both work?" I asked amiably.

"I don't know what those people do. And I have no interest in finding out."

"Thank you very much, Mrs. Crider. You've been very helpful."

"How did I help you?"

That was a good question. "I'm trying to get the chronology of events straight. Do you remember when you closed on your house?"

"Not the exact date. It was going to be the last of September, but we were able to get packed and get a mover a few days before that. The buyers were very anxious to get in quickly. I just don't remember the date anymore."

I thanked her again and got off the phone.

That left the mysterious Pasternaks. It wasn't likely that Mrs. Crider, who had lived next door to them on a fairly lonely road, knew nothing about them. Still, they could be people who preferred to be by themselves. But the voluble Mrs. Farragut had also declined to say anything about them. I had their phone number, and I dialed it, hoping I wouldn't trigger a barrage of criticism for invading their privacy.

After three rings I got an answering machine message asking me tersely to leave my name and number. I thought for a few seconds, then hung up. I would try again tomorrow.

"Anything new?" Jack asked when we sat down together.

"Nothing, I'm afraid. Laura has never heard of any of these names, and if one of these families knows something about Darby's disappearance, they're keeping it to themselves."

"What did you expect?"

"Maybe some reaction when I mention the name Filmore. But I watched them all carefully and there was nothing. I asked Laura about all the people we talked to today and she said she'd never heard of any of them."

"You asked her over the phone?"

"Yes."

"Maybe you should do it in person and watch her face, too."

I didn't like that. "Want to tell me why?"

"The Linton woman is taking you around, right?"

"Yes."

"So she's not afraid to be seen by any of the people you talk to up there."

"True."

"But if Laura Filmore is holding back on someone she knows in Connecticut, possibly someone in that area, you might notice something in her face if you hit the right button."

"I see."

"Have you given any thought to why her husband made that middle-of-the-night drive?"

"Since he kept it a secret, I assume it had to do with something he was involved in that he didn't want anyone to know about. Maybe he was in an automobile accident a few days before the party and he decided to settle it privately and not tell the police."

"So why did someone wake him up in the middle of the night?"

"Because . . . maybe someone at the other end took a turn for the worse or felt his pain was worth more than what they'd agreed on."

"Did the police note any damage to his car?"

I knew the answer to that one. Jack had seen the file over the weekend. "So it wasn't that. Maybe it was a youthful indiscretion come back to haunt him. People come out of the woodwork and make threats, don't they?"

"Let's push it a little," Jack said. "Does anyone care

anymore if a guy fathered an illegitimate child a long time ago?"

I sighed. "I suppose I would care, but no, the general population seems to have a high tolerance for that sort of thing nowadays."

"Same thing with an ex-wife."

"I hope you don't have one," I said.

"Why?"

That stumped me. I tried to think of a good reason. We're Catholic and he would have had to get a church annulment of his first marriage or our marriage would be invalid. He would have deceived me. He might be behind in alimony payments, and that's against the law. But if none of these situations existed, how terrible would it be if Jack had been married before we met? I couldn't imagine that he would be paying someone off to keep quiet about it. I said as much to him.

"If you can be forgiving about something like that, I would think Laura Filmore could, too. What I'm getting at is this: Whatever Larry Filmore left the house for after his birthday bash, it must have been something big, something that would really disgrace him, maybe a felony that wouldn't go away."

"And that includes murder," I said.

"Among other indiscretions."

"He did something," I said. "He got away with something. It could have happened just before the party or a long time before. And somebody knows or found out."

"And has evidence," Jack added. "Just knowing won't cut it. When Larry Filmore robbed the bank, he left something behind that was distinctly his, and now it's in the possession of a blackmailer."

"Very scary," I said.

"There could be signed documents, photographs of Larry with his hand in the till, so to speak."

"Or Larry Filmore standing over a body with a smoking gun."

"I think that's what you're dealing with, Chris."

"The question is: Does Laura know?"

"Don't know the answer to that. He could've confided in her or he could have decided to keep her out of it. In the first case, he told her where he was going when he left the house. In the second, he made up a story about trouble at the plant."

"And I have no way of knowing."

"You'll find out. Just keep at it."

I didn't have much choice.

12

While I was eager to talk to George Reilly, the cop who had lost the suicide weapon, I decided to go back to Connecticut on Tuesday and take Eddie with me. Although I wanted to do some more walking in the woods, I could put that off for another time. Today I would just knock on doors as Betty and I had done on Monday and continue to ask the same kinds of questions. I had Betty's maps and I knew how to get to the area, so it was just a matter of continuing along the roads that bordered the woods where Darby was lost.

Before we left, I got a call from Pat Damon, Ryan's mother, asking how Eddie was doing. I assured her that he was well over the problems the mysterious plague had visited on him. Apparently, she was working hard to find out what had caused the poisoning but still had no answer. I felt bad that she had such feelings of guilt and I told her I hadn't even thought about it for some time. Eddie was fine and I was sure the other children were also.

Then Eddie and I took off.

"We're going to visit the people in this house," I said to Eddie as I turned into a long driveway.

"Who are they?"

"Mr. And Mrs. Boynton," I said, reading from Betty's

list. We were still on the north end of the perimeter of the woods.

We got out of the car and went to the front door. A girl about twenty answered. When I spoke to her, she replied with a Scandinavian accent.

"Mrs. Boynton just came home," she said. "Maybe she has time to talk to you."

She left us in the front hall. The house was a large ranch, and I could hear voices from a room to the left. A few minutes later a good-looking woman appeared, a baby on her shoulder.

"I'm Grace Boynton."

"Hi. I'm Christine Bennett. This is my son, Eddie." I proceeded to ask whether she had lived here twelve years ago when Darby Maxwell disappeared.

"Let's sit down. Meta, can you take her? She'll probably sleep now."

The au pair took the baby and went off, cooing to her charge as she went. We walked into a very lived-in family room with toys scattered everywhere and made ourselves comfortable. Eddie found a lot of toys and sat down with them.

"I remember when that boy died," Grace Boynton said. "We hadn't lived here long. I was pregnant with my first child and I think I gave birth a day or two after his body was found. It was very upsetting."

"I can imagine. Did your husband take part in the search?"

"No. I think the volunteer firemen did. And some of the service organizations. He probably would have if I hadn't been so nervous about having my first child. She was a little late and I was afraid I'd go into labor and he wouldn't be here."

"I understand. Did you ever hear any talk over the years about that boy?"

"After it happened, there was a lot of talk, sympathetic talk. But that was all. Has something happened?"

I gave her the explanation for why I was looking into the tragedy.

"The boy died of exposure," she said. "I don't think there was any indication he'd been harmed."

"You're right; there wasn't. It's just that some new information has come to light. Tell me, do you know anyone named Pasternak that lives about a half mile from here?"

"Never heard of them."

"Have you ever known Larry Filmore and his wife, Laura?"

She thought a moment. "Can't say I have."

"The people next door to you, have they lived here long?"

"Two years. They built the house themselves. Took a long time doing it, maybe two or three years. They worked mostly weekends on it and vacations. They did quite a job."

"So they wouldn't have been here twelve years ago."

"They lived somewhere else in Connecticut; I forget where."

"Thank you, Mrs. Boynton." I got up and told Eddie it was time to go.

"What new information is there about the retarded boy?" she asked.

"We think he may have spent some time in someone's house during the days he was missing."

"You mean he was kept somewhere against his will?"

"Possibly."

"That's very frightening. I don't know what your information is, but a lot of houses around here have an old barn out back or a caretaker's house or an artist's studio. Maybe the boy just went into a building like that to get out of the cold. No one may even have known he was there."

"That's possible. I guess I should be looking for barns and studios."

"You should," she said. "They're all over the place."

We left and I drove down the road, not bothering to stop at the two-year-old house that was next on the road. What Mrs. Boynton had said was true; a lot of houses around here, especially older ones, had an additional structure, sometimes two, on the property. As we drove by the new house next to hers, I noticed that they had also built some kind of little hut that could be used for storage or painting or just daydreaming. I tried to remember if any of the houses we had seen yesterday had had such structures. Before we left today, I would have to drive by them again and see.

We went down the road and stopped at all the houses. Half of them were empty; several hadn't been built twelve years ago; three of them had barns or cottages behind them. No one I spoke to had ever heard of the Filmores. Everyone who had lived here when Darby disappeared remembered what had happened. Eddie got fidgety and I couldn't blame him. If you look at the world through the eyes of a three- or four-year-old, you realize how strange certain events can seem. Mommy goes for a drive, stops at every house, asks a lot of questions, goes back to the car. What is Mommy looking for? She could knock on doors in our town if she wanted to.

Where there were barns and cottages, I asked if I could see them. One was a faded old red barn. There was still hay inside and stalls for horses. The owner, an elderly woman named Mrs. Pinker, said they owned horses for a while after the war when her children were young. She meant World War II. Had the barn been used for anything else since? I asked. Just as an extra garage and to store garden equipment.

I thought that if I were lost and found a place like this, I might go inside to get out of the cold and wind, although it wasn't much milder inside than out.

"Where are the horses?" Eddie asked, having heard Mrs. Pinker mention them.

"They're gone," I said.

"Where did they go?"

"I think the lady gave them away. Nobody was riding them anymore."

"Poor horses," Eddie said.

We had lunch at the same place Betty and I had gone to yesterday. The waitress remembered me and took an interest in Eddie. While they were chatting, I checked my notes. One house had had a caretaker's cottage that was rented out to a young couple. They weren't home and the owner wouldn't unlock the door. I asked who had lived there before the current residents, and she said from time to time they rented it to a single person or a couple, but she couldn't give me dates or years. It was obviously off the books, and no records were kept. Once, she said, they had rented to a couple with a small child and they wouldn't do that again. She didn't explain and I didn't ask.

One other house had had a barn, not a big old one that had housed animals but more of a shed that a daughter had used as a writer's studio. Going through the notes I had taken, I had a rush of admiration for the police who did this work on a regular basis. They, of course, had more power than I. They could get inside a locked cottage if they had to, but it was a tedious job and often yielded as little as my work had.

After lunch I drove back to the Pasternaks' house. This time I was pretty sure there was someone home. Smoke was coming out of the chimney. We walked up to the front door and I rang the bell.

"Who is it?" a woman's voice called from inside.

"My name is Christine Bennett!" I called back.

"What do you want?"

"I'd like to talk to you!"

"What are you selling?"

"I'm not selling anything!" I was getting tired of shouting.

"That's what everyone says."

I waited, but nothing happened. "Mrs. Pasternak?" I called.

The door was pulled open. The woman standing there, giving us a hostile look, had graying hair pulled back in a bun. She was wearing a loose brown jumper with a brown turtleneck sweater and heavy shoes. Her eyes were dark and piercing. I felt Eddie's hand tighten on my own. I didn't blame him.

"Yes?" she said.

"Mrs. Pasternak, I'm looking for information about the young man who died in the woods twelve years ago. Darby Maxwell. Do you remember that?"

"Should I?"

"Most of the people around here recall what happened. He was lost in the woods. A lot of the men were part of the search."

"He was retarded."

"That's right. If you have a minute, I'd like to talk to you about it."

She stood there looking at us, and I wondered whether she was going to make us stand in the cold or close the door in our faces. Finally she said, "Come inside."

We went in and stood in the foyer. It was warm inside, which was all I cared about. Eddie stayed very close to me and said nothing.

"I can't tell you anything," she said, preempting my questions.

"I wondered if you ever heard any gossip about that young man, if he might have stayed with someone in the area."

"I don't gossip."

I could believe it. "Well, perhaps—"

"I remember the incident. I don't know any more about it than what I read in the papers."

This was not going to be a productive interview and I didn't think being warm and friendly would alter her demeanor. I got to the point. "Have you ever known anyone named Filmore?"

"Filmore?"

"Yes. A man named Lawrence and his wife, Laura."

"Lawrence Filmore." For the first time, she seemed to have an interest in my question. "It rings a bell," she said, an almost-smile working around her hard mouth. "But not because I ever knew anyone with that name. I grew up in Buffalo and there's a Fillmore Avenue there, a big street. It's named after the president, you know. He was a Buffalo man."

"I see," I said, feeling disappointed.

"I don't think I can help you."

"Do you have a barn or studio behind your house?"

"We did when we moved in, but we took it down. It was rotting."

"When was that?"

"Must be twenty years ago."

"Thank you, Mrs. Pasternak."

She smiled suddenly, looking at Eddie. "Bye-bye, little boy."

"Bye," Eddie said. He was glad to get out of there.

I drove down the road looking for second structures behind houses. Where the Criders had lived there was none; where Mrs. Farragut lived there was none. Then I tried the first road Betty and I had covered. Behind Alice Warren's house there was nothing, but next door, where her daughter, Michelle Franklin, lived, there was a building about the size of a two-car garage.

"This is our last stop, Eddie," I said as I turned into the driveway.

"Can we go home?"

"Right after I ask this lady a question."

Michelle Franklin opened the door and invited us in. We went into the kitchen, where she had cookies for Eddie, who was now glad we had made the stop.

"I have just one quick question," I said. "The building out back, how long has that been there?"

"Not long. We built it about five years ago, maybe six. I dabble in watercolors. I'm not very good, but I like doing it. My husband uses half of it for his gardening things and tools for the car. My half is where I paint. We don't even have a heating system, just a plug-in heater, but it's nice for me."

"So you're sure it wasn't there when Darby Maxwell was lost in the woods?"

"Twelve years ago? Not a chance. I can get you the date we built it if it's important."

"That's OK. I'll take your word for it."

With an extra cookie wrapped in a napkin, we went out to the car. I took a quick look behind the Gallaghers' house, saw nothing, and drove home.

"Kind of a wasted day," I said to Jack that night. "Nobody flinches when I mention the name Filmore and there's no way of telling whether an old barn once housed a young man for a night or two."

"I suppose forensics could give it a try."

"Twelve years later? It's a massive job."

"Cheer up. It's always the last guy you question who gives the answer you're looking for."

"True. But I think tomorrow I'll drive down to the city and look up George Reilly in Brooklyn."

"Sounds like a good idea, but I don't think it'll lead anywhere. He'll tell you he lost the gun in the snow and it really cost him. But it's a base that needs touching."

I agreed. I had already arranged for Elsie to keep Eddie after my morning class. Taking him to Connecticut today had not been one of my better ideas.

13

My class Wednesday morning was quite lively. This year, for the first time, I had several male students, and they changed the rhythm of the class. One of them slept through most of the classes, but the others contributed and often had points of view provocatively different from the women's. One of them frequently insisted that whatever the title of the course, we should read at least one good, solid detective novel written by a man. He reiterated his feelings again this morning.

"Let's take a vote," I said.

The women overwhelmingly agreed and even the sleeper woke up long enough to raise one arm.

"OK. I'm agreeable. Do you have a suggestion or do you want me to pick the book?"

"Something tough," Barry Woodson said.

"Give me a name."

"Block," he said. "Lawrence Block. One of the Scudder books. I've read a lot of them. They're really cool."

"Fine," I said. "How about *Eight Million Ways to Die*?"

"Sure."

"Let's add it to the list. Can you have it read in two weeks?"

There was a collective groan. I've learned not to take such things too seriously. Leave it to the students and the syllabus will include one seventy-five-page-long novella and a lot of deep thought.

"Two weeks," I said. "Now let's get back to Christie."

As I usually do after my class, I had a good lunch in the cafeteria, then drove into New York. Jack had shown me how to get to the station house where George Reilly spent his days. I hadn't been to Brooklyn for some time and it was rather nice revisiting it. It was at the Sixty-fifth Precinct that I had first met Jack while I was looking into a forty-year-old murder that took place on Good Friday in 1950. I didn't expect anything quite that exciting to happen today.

I had to park a few blocks away because the streets were full. I walked back and went inside, waiting till some business was taken care of at the desk. Then I went over and talked to a remarkably young-looking sergeant.

"I'm looking for George Reilly," I said.

"Lemme check." He made a call and came back. "He's in. Hey, Mario, you got a minute to take this lady down to the property locker?"

"Sure, Sarge." Mario was also young, an officer in uniform. He came over and said, "Right this way."

We went downstairs, and when we got to the property locker it turned out to be a room with an old-style two-piece Dutch door, separated in the middle by a scarred shelf. The interior was wire cages floor to ceiling. When we got to the door, he called for George, who was probably taking a postprandial nap. There were some grunts and yawns and a stocky, graying middle-aged cop came to the window.

"Thanks," I said to Mario. "Officer Reilly, I'm Christine Bennett. I'd like to ask you about something that happened several years ago."

"You a cop?"

"No. I'm looking into a pair of mysterious deaths that happened twelve years ago and involved people living in my town. One of the victims was shot with a gun that once belonged to you."

"Not that again," he said, visibly unnerved.

"Do you know about this death?"

"It got back to me."

"I wonder if you would tell me how you lost that gun."

He sighed audibly. "You know, I been through this so many times—"

"I know you have, and I apologize for bothering you again." I resisted the impulse to say I knew he was very busy. "But I've discovered something connected to that death—"

"It was a suicide, right?"

"An apparent suicide, yes. We have no idea where the victim got the gun or if it was even his, and I just want to go over your end of it one more time."

"It's all in the record, but here goes. It was February of '69. I was assigned to the Two-Six in Harlem and the snow was like unbelievable. It's the worst storm I ever saw. I was out on the street because a call came in about a disturbance in one of the tenements there. We could hardly get up the front steps, there was so much snow already. We went inside and rang the bell to the apartment. It was on the fifth floor. They're always on the fifth floor," he added. "I don't think I ever had a call on the first or second. Anyhow, they didn't answer, so my partner rang another bell and we got buzzed in. We went up, knocked on the door, announced ourselves, but there wasn't a sound. We knocked on the next door and a girl opened up and said she'd heard something, but she thought they'd gone out. You gotta remember, this was a long time before the modern nine-one-one. Nowadays, nine-one-one knows where you're callin' from.

If someone called the police and didn't give a name and number, we had no way of finding that out back then."

"So you didn't know if the girl who answered the door had called or someone in the apartment you were told to go to."

"You got it. Anyways, we didn't have a reason to bust the door down, so we didn't. We asked downstairs did anyone hear anything up on five, and no one heard. Or they said they didn't. So we went back down to the street, walked down the front steps—you couldn't even see where we'd walked up ten or fifteen minutes ago, that's how hard it was snowing—and some guy came out of the shadows and jumped me."

"That must have been terrible," I said.

"Lemme tell you." He nodded his head and I could almost sense him remembering that night, the cold, the snow, the shock of the sudden attack. "Anyway, I went for my gun. My partner, meanwhile, he was jumped by another guy, so he was no good to me. While I was trying to pop the holster, this guy gives me a chop on my wrist with somethin'; I thought he broke it. He was on my back, you understand, a big, heavy hulk of a guy. I know I screamed when he chopped me. Next thing I know, I'm lying in the snow, the guy is gone, and my gun is gone."

"What about your partner?"

"My partner was luckier. He got the other guy off his back and then the two of them took off. We couldn't see them three seconds after they started to run. My partner didn't chase them 'cause he thought I was hurt and he didn't know about my gun."

"It sounds to me like all they wanted was the gun."

"That's the way I figure it. We spent some time there kickin' around the snow to see if my gun was there, but we never found it. We called the precinct and they sent a sergeant and then later the duty captain came and some other cops to search. We went back to the house and I made out a UF-sixty-one report and the duty captain interviewed me."

"How long was the snow on the ground?" I asked.

"Weeks. They limited traffic because they couldn't clean it up. In Queens there was almost a revolution."

"Why?" I asked innocently.

"When there's a lot of snow, they don't plow Queens till every other place in the city is taken care of. That's just the way it is," he said, accepting life in New York as New Yorkers knew it. "The mayor took a lotta flak about that, but hey, he got reelected. People got short memories."

"Are you sure the man who attacked you took the gun or is it possible it just got dropped in the snow?"

"Anything's possible. It was night; you couldn't see. If the gun dropped, it would've gone right through the snow and got buried. We were all over the place, stomping around to get these mutts off of us. All I know is, when they ran, I didn't have my gun."

"Were you able to describe the men who attacked you?"

"They were on our backs; we never saw them. Black, what can I tell you? Both black, one pretty big, one not so big. We went down the street about a minute after the fight, but they were long gone. They coulda ducked into an alley, another tenement, and come out on the next block."

I didn't think I could get much more out of him. "Thank you, Officer Reilly. I appreciate your taking the time to talk to me."

"You know, I paid for that loss. I got a complaint, went to the trial room, and lost five days' pay. No deal, they said. That really hurt. And I had to buy another gun besides."

"I'm sure it did. Well, at least it's nice and warm in here."

"Right. I couldn't ask for better."

I drove back home and picked up Eddie at Elsie's. She

was planning to bake a wonderful cake for his birthday and wanted to know if I had arranged a date for the party. It was just a few weeks away and I knew I'd better get started and send out invitations. We looked at the calendar and figured out a date. Then I drove us home.

When we'd taken off our coats, I called Mel.

"Hey, I haven't seen you guys for a while. Feel like coming over?"

"I was going to invite you."

"Nah, come over here. I just put the heat up. No reason to heat up two houses, right?"

I laughed. She knew how careful I was with money. I always put the heat down when I left, and she was right: why heat two houses? And Eddie always enjoyed going over there.

It was nice and warm when we walked in. Mel teaches and comes home when the kids do, so she'd been there for half an hour or so. She scooted Eddie upstairs to play with her children and we did our usual, making tea and sitting in the family room.

"So what's new in your life?" Mel asked when we were comfortable.

I told her what I had learned about Laura's husband and Betty's son.

"Let me understand this. You put two accidental deaths in two different places together because of the sneakers the victims were wearing?"

"It was a lucky coincidence that I read the letters in my aunt's box of memorabilia and then got in touch with the survivors. Everyone thought Darby was lost in the woods and died of exposure because he couldn't find his way back. And it appeared that Laura's husband shot himself. And maybe he did. But sometime between when he left his house after his big birthday party and when he was shot in his garage, he and Darby Maxwell met."

"Amazing. So why did they trade sneakers, or don't you know that yet?"

"I don't know anything for sure, but my theory is that they were both held against their will for a while by a person who may have known Larry Filmore and may have just come across Darby Maxwell. If Filmore had a feeling that this was all going to end up badly, he wanted to make sure that something would be wrong on both the bodies so that it would be obvious that the deaths weren't accidental."

"Brilliant," Mel said.

"Brilliant of him. Only no one noticed the wrong sneakers until sometime later and it didn't seem important enough to tell the police. The women assumed it was some kind of mistake or mix-up. You know, the people in the medical examiner's office get very defensive when they think you're accusing them of stealing something. All the clothing and other possessions were inventoried, so it would be foolish for someone at the end of the line to make a switch and keep something for himself."

"But it was no mistake and that changes everything."

"Right."

"What does Laura Filmore have to say about all this?"

"She came to Connecticut with me last Friday and met Betty Linton. I had hoped we'd find some person that they both knew, but it didn't work out. Still, both women are now convinced that there was some kind of foul play involved in the deaths."

"This is very creepy, Chris."

"I only hope I can find out what went on. Tell me, have you ever heard any scuttlebutt about Laura's husband?"

"Never. I told you, we didn't live here twelve years ago. You'll have to ask one of the old-timers in town. But it might get back to Laura."

"I've thought of that. I'm sure she wouldn't appreciate my trying to dig up dirt about her husband."

"You think there is any?"

"There has to be. Somebody called him in the middle of the night."

"Maybe Laura lied about that."

"Then why did he leave the house? I agree she may have lied about part of it. Maybe he didn't tell her he was going to the plant because there was a problem. Maybe he said, 'I'm going to see so-and-so in Connecticut because he's making my life miserable.' But I doubt it. If he was going to see so-and-so, he'd have done it during the day or the middle of some other night. That just wasn't the right night for him to go anywhere."

"I think you've convinced me. But she may know where he went."

"Yes, she may."

"And that means she's holding back. But why would she do that, Chris? Even if she lied the morning after he disappeared, she would have gotten pretty worried when he didn't come back. If she knew where he was going, wouldn't she have told the police?"

"I think she would have. I really think this woman loved her husband. She didn't run away with anyone else after he died."

"And she didn't run out and spend a lot of his money," Mel put in. "She stayed in the same house; she worked at the same things. And she's a wonderful volunteer at the school. She is so good with the kids. I have to tell you, I really like her."

I had the same feelings about Laura myself, although I didn't know her very well. But I was glad to hear Mel stand up for her. "So the chances are she didn't lie about where her husband went. He told her one thing and did another."

"He was protecting her."

"From what?"

"If I knew that, I'd know who was responsible for his death."

I did a lot of thinking that night. I hadn't learned much from my two days in Connecticut. No one I'd talked to, including Mrs. Pasternak, seemed at all suspicious. You couldn't haul people in for questioning because they had a barn or shed behind their house that Darby and Larry Filmore might have spent a night in twelve years ago. I still had a number of houses on the map that I hadn't driven by, most of them to the northwest of the last place Darby was seen. And I hadn't yet seen the pond that Betty had mentioned, which had been searched on the chance he had drowned in it. But I thought I needed to know more about Larry Filmore and it took me a while to think of someone I could ask.

The next morning, I called Celia Yaeger and asked if we could speak again. She invited me over and I decided to leave Eddie with Elsie, as I recalled that Mrs. Yaeger's house was quite elegant, with breakables everywhere you turned, and I thought it would be smart to avoid a catastrophe.

I arrived at one-thirty as planned and she asked me once again if I would join her for a glass of sherry. This time I turned her down and she didn't take one for herself. We sat in the living room and made small talk for a few minutes. She seemed to be on top of all the local gossip, and she knew I had been in touch with Laura and that we had been out to Connecticut.

"You certainly move fast," she said.

"I really want to find out what happened. Two people died very horrible and unnecessary deaths. If someone was responsible for one or both of those deaths, he should be brought to justice."

"You're certainly right about that. How do you think I can help you?"

I was a little less sure of myself at that moment than I had been when I walked inside her house. If she was in constant touch with Laura, anything I asked had a good chance of getting back to her, and that was what I had hoped to avoid. But I was convinced this woman knew everything there was to know about townspeople.

"This is a little awkward," I said. "I'd like to ask you some questions in absolute confidence."

"I will keep your questions to myself, but I reserve the right not to answer them."

"Fair enough. I've been giving a lot of thought to why Larry Filmore got a phone call in the middle of the night twelve years ago and drove away immediately."

"I understand he told Laura there was trouble at the plant, but it turned out he hadn't gone there and there wasn't any trouble."

"That's right. He went somewhere else, maybe to several places, but one of the places he went was Connecticut."

"How very strange."

"Mrs. Yaeger, there must have been some secret in his life, something very threatening, enough to make him get out of bed and drive a distance when he was told to. Do you have any idea what that secret could have been?"

"No idea at all. Of course, everyone who knew Larry must have pondered why he took his life. If anyone came up with an answer, I don't know about it. I never thought of a reason."

"Was there any gossip?"

"I don't listen to gossip." It was a strange thing for this woman to say. It was clear she knew everything that was going on, but I assumed she didn't consider that to be gossip. "There was lots of speculation after Larry died.

Most of it had to do with whether he was in financial trouble, but the business has thrived. If Laura discovered that he had debts of any sort, gambling debts or the like, she's kept it to herself. And let me add, I don't think there were any."

"You know," I said, "there are other kinds of secrets in people's lives. When I was a youngster, I remember hearing that a meteorologist on the radio who called himself 'Doctor' didn't really have a doctorate after all. Someone wrote to the station, someone who knew him years before, and told them. They investigated and found the charge to be true. The man lost his job."

"I see what you're saying. You think Larry may have lied about something in his past and someone was blackmailing him about it."

"Something on that order."

"Well, I didn't know him when he was a boy. He and Laura bought their house here after they were married. I assume the police looked into his past when he died."

"I'm sure they did, and I know they didn't find anything. But there's always the possibility . . ." I let it hang, hoping she would follow my line of thought.

"He could have married someone under a different name; he could have fathered a child before his marriage."

"Those are the kinds of things."

"I don't know of anything like that, Chris. And I can tell you honestly, I never heard a whisper about such things. I know Laura quite well and I spent a lot of time with her after what happened. If she had fears of anything in her husband's life becoming public, she never told me."

"Well, I guess that's it then. It looks like a dead end."

"But it isn't a dead end," she said briskly. "You're on the right track. Either Larry killed himself because of some secret he never shared, or he was killed for some reason we don't know about and it was made to look like suicide. I wish I knew how you could find out what that is."

"So do I." I stood and picked up my bag. It had been a long shot, but I couldn't leave these questions unasked. "Thank you for being so cooperative."

"There is one thing I can do," she said. "Before you go, give me a minute. Let me see if I can find it." She left the room and went upstairs.

I waited in the living room, wondering what she was looking for. She was gone for several minutes. When she came down the stairs, she was holding a small bag.

"I was the self-appointed photographer at the birthday party," she said. "I owned a good camera and I came with a few rolls of film. The Filmores didn't want a professional photographer at the party and they were pleased when I volunteered my services. For me, it was a pleasure. I didn't know everyone there, but I went from table to table taking pictures, talking to the guests. I really enjoyed it. I got some good ones of Larry and Laura. What I intended to do was make an album and give it to them as a gift, but after what happened, I didn't even have the film developed for a long time. I'm not sure I've ever really looked at all the photos." She handed the bag to me. "The film envelopes are in here. I doubt whether you'll learn anything of interest, but why don't you give it a try?"

"Thank you very much. I will certainly look at all the pictures. Has Laura seen them?"

"No. I didn't have the heart to show them to her. She never asked about them and I just put them away. That's what took me so long upstairs. I wasn't sure where they were. It's been so long."

"Are they labeled?" I asked.

"No, but you'll recognize Laura, and the man with her is Larry. If you have any questions, she'd be the one to ask. She knew everyone there; I didn't."

I shook hands with Celia and went home, the little bag on the seat beside me. Like Celia, I didn't think I'd learn anything, but it was worth an hour to find out.

14

Since Eddie was taken care of for the afternoon, I went home and took the pictures out of the bag. There were two envelopes of over thirty pictures each, all of them enlarged to four-by-six, so they were easy to inspect. Most of them were quite boring, one table after another of people gathered along one side so they all fit in the picture. Everyone looked ridiculously happy. Everyone was dressed elegantly. The one picture that sent a shock wave through me was the one with my aunt. She looked so healthy, so happy, so vibrant. She was such an important person in my life, filling in for my parents when they died, that I feel her loss to this day.

I looked at every picture of every table. Finally, I found a group of pictures of the Filmores. Laura looked radiant, her dress surely an expensive designer model. The man beside her was good-looking, healthy-looking, and appeared to be as happy as one would expect at such an occasion. Their children appeared in a couple of pictures with them and also other people who obviously wanted a picture of themselves with the birthday man.

I kept the clearest photo of Larry Filmore on the table and started looking for him in other pictures. He hadn't gone to the tables to be photographed, but he was at the head table next to his wife and several people I did not know, one of them almost certainly his mother. He was eating, talking, standing behind someone, and pointing at something on the table. In one picture, he was looking to his right at a man who was not dressed as a guest but was standing just behind the people who were seated and leaning over toward Larry. It looked as though Larry was being told something or asked something. I got a magnifying glass and held it over the picture. The man carrying the message looked vaguely familiar, but where had I seen him? I held the glass as steady as I could and looked at his face. His hair was shaggy and he had a mustache. He was wearing what might have been work clothes.

And then it dawned on me. He was the janitor at our church. I got up and put my coat on. Taking the photos, I went out to the car and drove to the church.

There were no classes or meetings this afternoon and the building was very quiet. I went to the main office, but it was locked. The confessionals were empty and the priest was nowhere to be found. I started looking in the classrooms and meeting rooms, but one after the other they were empty. Finally, I found my way down to the furnace room. The door was open.

I stuck my head in and called, "Hello!"

"Yeah?" The voice came from behind the boiler, but its owner emerged a moment later. "Oh, Mrs. Brooks. You looking for me?"

"I think so. I'd like you to look at a picture. Is this you, Roger?"

He put on a pair of glasses and took the picture from me. "Look at that," he said with a smile. "That musta been taken a long time ago. Look at all the hair I had."

"Twelve years ago. That was Mr. Filmore's birthday party."

"Ah. I remember now. What a party that was. What a terrible thing happened afterward. You weren't here then, were you?"

"No. I moved to Oakwood about half a dozen years ago. My aunt lived here, Margaret Wirth. She was at the party."

"Mrs. Wirth, yeah. Nice lady. Always had a good word for everyone."

"Roger, that's you and that's Mr. Filmore. Do you remember why you came into the party to talk to him?"

"Sure, I remember. He got a phone call."

"At the church? How could that be?"

"I got no idea. I just know I was sittin' upstairs watchin' TV and the phone rang and a guy asked for Mr. Filmore."

"So you went and got him," I said.

"I went down to the ballroom, went over to the table, told him he had a phone call, and left."

"And what did he do?"

"He followed me out. He went up to the office and picked up the phone."

"Did he talk long?"

"A coupla minutes."

"Did you hear what he said?"

Roger gave me a look.

"I don't mean were you listening in on the call. I mean, you were there and maybe you heard something."

"He told the guy to leave him alone. He said he was busy. He said, 'I'll call you tomorrow.' "

"Did you tell that to the police?"

"No. Why should I?"

"I just wondered if they questioned you."

"About what?"

"Mr. Filmore committed suicide. I thought maybe the police talked to people who had been at the party."

"They didn't talk to me."

"Thank you, Roger. You've been a big help."

I went to the pay phone and called Laura. She wasn't home, so I took a chance and drove to the school. When I got there, I walked through the parking lot till I found her car. The children were just getting out, so I stood near the car till I saw her.

"Chris. Are you looking for me?"

"Yes. I want to talk to you about something that happened at the happy birthday party."

Her face clouded. "It's cold here. Can we drive to my house?"

"Sure. I'll take my car."

She pulled into her driveway first and then into the garage, using her remote door opener. I parked in the driveway and we went inside together.

When we had our coats off, I told her I had talked to Celia, who had given me the pictures taken at the party.

"The pictures," she said, as though it were a revelation. "I forgot all about the pictures. She was our photographer that night."

"That's what she told me." I took out the photo of Roger talking to her husband.

"Oh, look at that," she said. "There's Larry's mother on the left. I'm not there. I must have been talking to guests. Is that Roger? What's he doing there?"

"Just what I asked. I've just been to see him. He was telling your husband he had a phone call."

She seemed stunned. "Someone called him at the party?"

"You didn't know?"

"He never said a word. Do you know who it was?"

"A man. Roger heard the conversation, or part of it. He was a little embarrassed. He thought I'd think he was eavesdropping. He heard your husband say," I looked at my notebook, "he wanted to be left alone. He said he was busy. He said, 'I'll call you tomorrow.'"

"I never knew anything about this," Laura said almost in a whisper.

"My question is this: How did this person know to call your husband at the church?"

"I don't know." She thought about it, her brow furrowed. "Maybe—oh, I know. Larry put the church number on call forwarding. In case there was a problem at the plant, they would be able to reach him. He did that all the time."

"So the person calling didn't know where Larry was."

"No. He probably called the house and it rang at the church. But this is amazing, Chris. It means the person who called in the middle of the night may have called earlier that night."

"And Larry never told you?"

"He never said a word. I couldn't even tell you what time this happened, but I can give you a range. We started with cocktails at seven and then we all sat down about eight for the dinner. There's food on the table, see? I bet we were finishing our main course when I left the table to walk around and talk to people. Larry was sitting with his mother. She was a slow eater and I'm sure he stayed till she was finished. So I'd guess the call came in about nine o'clock, maybe a little earlier."

"And he was probably back at the table when you got back for dessert."

"I suppose so. Since I had no idea he had left."

"Laura, think back. Did your husband get phone calls that he tried to keep secret from you?"

"Chris, Larry got calls all the time. He worked on committees for charities and museums and service organizations. We had a second phone line put into the house long before people started getting a fax line or a line for the computer. When his phone rang, he often took it in his office at home. I never asked who it was or what it was about, because it didn't interest me. If he thought I would want to know, he told me. I didn't tell him every time one of my friends or organizations called."

"I understand."

"But this is very interesting." She looked at the picture again. "He looks concerned, doesn't he?" she said with the knowledge of how the events had played out so long ago. "If only he'd told me."

"Laura, let's assume something happened in his life that could have brought embarrassment to him. Think back to the time before you had two phone lines and before you were both involved in your projects. Do you remember being curious then about mysterious phone calls?"

"There were no mysterious phone calls. And we didn't have an unlisted number. Anyone could have looked us up in the book and called us."

"And you never had any sense that something peculiar was going on in his life?"

"Never."

"Did you ever get strange or threatening calls on your line?"

"Nothing besides wrong numbers. No heavy breathing, none of the calls women sometimes complain about."

"Did you have separate answering machines?" I asked.

"I had one. Larry didn't. He felt if it was important, they'd call back. And he forwarded his calls when we went out."

So no one could leave a threatening message that Mrs. Filmore might hear when she came home. Perhaps that was by design. "And your husband was in the book, too, I suppose."

"Well." She looked a little sheepish. "Actually, mine was unlisted. Larry thought it was safer that way. We had two very different numbers. They didn't roll into one another."

"And after he died, what did you do about his phone number?"

"I kept it. Mostly the telemarketers call that one now. And my kids know they can reach me on that one if my line is busy and they need me. It's still listed and mine is still unlisted. Why do you ask?"

"I just wondered whether the person he went to see that night might have called after your husband died."

"I would have told the police," Laura said. "No one called, not on his phone and not on mine."

"So either he gave up or he felt it was too dangerous to pursue whatever it was he was after."

"Or it was moot," Laura said. "If Larry was involved in something, and I don't for a minute believe he was, after he was dead, it could do much less harm."

"I guess so. Well, I have the rest of the pictures if you'd like to look at them. But I'd like to keep them for the time being." I handed her the bag.

She pulled out the envelopes and started through them. As she scanned them, small sounds came from her, as though these reminders were alternately painful and pleasant. Occasionally she smiled. Suddenly I saw a tear drop on the table. She brushed her eyes and continued till she had seen all the photos. Then she gave them back.

"It's very hard," she said. "Many of the people there are gone now. Your aunt is one of them. Larry's mother is another. She never recovered from the shock of her son killing himself. It just broke her."

"I'm sorry this has been so painful."

"But you're learning things, Chris. I wish I could tell you more."

"Were your parents at the party?"

"They died years before."

"No brothers and sisters?"

She smiled. "I was a spoiled only child."

"From where?"

"Wisconsin."

"Cold winters," I said.

"Very. But good cheese."

I collected the photos and went to Elsie's to pick up Eddie. He was in a good mood, as he always is when he visits her. We all sat for a bit and talked. It's very relaxing to be with Elsie. She's a woman who is very comfortable in her life. There were times when she worked, times when she stayed home with her children, even a time when she did both for a while. Now she has added being a surrogate grandmother to her list of accomplishments, and I marvel at how good she is at it. Sometimes I wonder if I will miraculously learn to cook wonderful foods and bake marvelous cookies by the time I reach that point in my own life. But with an almost-four-year-old, I have some time to work on those skills myself.

"That's a nice discovery," Jack said that evening.

"But all it tells me is that someone called him, someone he didn't want to talk to. It doesn't tell me who it was or why he called."

"You know it's a man now."

"True. One small step."

"And Laura claims she had no idea this guy was calling her husband?"

I explained about the two phone lines, the many calls, the lack of an answering machine. "You don't ask me who I'm talking to every time I pick up the phone."

"True. And with two lines, they could both be on the phone at the same time."

I sighed. "I think our house is complete with one phone line."

"OK with me. So what's next?"

"There are still houses I haven't been to. And I've only walked through a small part of the area Darby may have covered in Connecticut."

"I don't want you getting lost."

"I have a compass, remember? That should keep me from going in circles."

"Wish I could keep from going in circles. Maybe I'll take a compass to work with me tomorrow."

15

I decided, much as I didn't want to do it, to make what I hoped would be a last trip to Connecticut to interview people at houses I had not yet visited and those where no one had been home earlier in the week. I called Celia before I left and told her how useful the photos had been. She was surprised and told me to keep them as long as I wanted.

I drove the now familiar roads, observing that the leaves were practically gone. It was a gray day with a bleak sky, too soon for snow and a little too warm. I was glad. I didn't need icy roads on a long drive.

I spent what was left of the morning going from house to house on Betty's map. It was very much the usual. Everyone who had lived there twelve years ago remembered what had happened. No one knew anything beyond the obvious. There were sheds and barns and caretakers' cottages, many of them in place for decades, but no way of knowing whether Darby had stopped in one voluntarily or had been held in one against his will. I had a sense of despair, a feeling that I would never crack the shell around whoever might be lying to me. How could I? These all seemed to be nice, ordinary people who lived, worked, cared for their children, took part in search parties, and moved south when the winter weather got to be too much for them. Even the Pasternaks, whom their neighbors seemed to want to avoid, had turned out to be within the norm, or at least as far as *I* could see they were. What was I going to learn that would give me the insight I wanted?

Usually at this stage of an investigation I would meet with Sister Joseph, my dearest friend and General Superior at St. Stephen's. I put my facts on the table, ask for and receive her take on the mystery that has me befuddled, and then, following the way she has pointed, go on my way to wind it up. But what did I have that I could tell her? That I had interviewed most of the residents of twenty-some houses, all of whom claimed to know nothing that would help me? What could she possibly suggest on the basis of such flimsy facts?

I went to lunch and opened my notebook on the table, reading my scribblings as I ate. It was clear to me that Larry Filmore had a secret he was keeping from the world and probably, but not definitely, from his wife as well. It all seemed so well thought out. His line and her line. Her answering machine, but none for him. Her line is unlisted, so she never gets a call from the person who is blackmailing her husband. Or whatever he was doing to her husband.

As my eye moved down the pages in my book, the name Charlie Calhoun popped out at me. Charlie was the night watchman at the Filmore plant. It struck me that I didn't know where he lived. He had been so positive about Larry Filmore, I had mentally deleted him from my list of suspects, not that I had such a list. But should I have dismissed him so quickly? Living where we do on the Long Island Sound, we are not far from Connecticut. Where Betty lives is quite a drive, but it was possible that Charlie lived somewhere up there. The plant was in New York State, but I recalled driving toward Connecticut to reach it. It was worth a try. Maybe Larry Filmore had done something at work that Charlie knew about and no one else did.

When I finished eating, I drove to the house Betty and her son had been visiting when Darby disappeared. I rang the doorbell, but no one answered, so I started walking. I got into the woods and pulled my compass out of my coat pocket to get my bearings. I continued north, as Betty had taken us a week ago. I remembered how fearful Laura and I had become on the way back when it looked as though Betty had lost her way. I felt fairly confident now with my little aid in my hand and I pushed through, looking for the clearing we had reached. On the map, it was due north of the house I had just left.

The walk seemed to take longer than a week ago, but I had neglected to check my watch when I began, so I had no way of being certain. Finally, I came out under the murky sky. I looked all around to see whether any houses or backyards were visible from here, but I could find none. I pressed on.

After about five minutes, I came to the pond. It was larger than I had imagined and easy to stumble into. The water looked dark, not very appetizing. I saw something white lying on the foliage on the far side and I walked around to see what it was. It was a wool scarf with fringe. Someone had left it or lost it here. It was still clean, so I assumed it hadn't been lying there for very long.

I checked my compass and decided to turn east. If Darby had drifted to his right, this is where he would have gone. Ahead of me were more woods, and as I was about to enter them I heard girlish laughter from somewhere behind me. I turned to see a teenage girl and boy running toward the pond.

"Hey, miss!" the boy called.

"Hi!" I called back.

"Did you see a white scarf anywhere around here?"

"It's over there by the pond!" I pointed toward the west.

The girl started laughing loudly. "Thank you!" she called to me. "Race you," she said to the boy, and they took off, the boy charging ahead of her.

I watched as they rounded the pond, saw the scarf, and ran toward it. As they reached it, they collapsed on the ground, the boy kissing her hungrily. I turned back to the woods, pretty sure I knew how the scarf had been lost in the first place.

I decided to spend another fifteen minutes walking through the woods on the north. I didn't know which way Darby's friend had led him through the woods, which way he began to walk when he found himself alone. Had he drifted right or left? Had he come to the pond? I was feeling pretty cold by then, my toes especially, even though I was wearing warm socks and leather boots. Poor Darby had been dressed in shorts on that warm day twelve years ago. Every step I took reminded me how alone he must have felt, how terribly cold at night.

I was just ready to turn back when I thought I saw a house through the trees. I kept going and then I saw it clearly. It was the back of the Pasternaks' house.

"You had to come out somewhere," Jack said when I finished my story. "You couldn't keep walking through the woods and not hit a house eventually."

"Unless I walked in circles."

"But you were carrying a compass. You knew where you were going."

"Even with the compass I didn't walk straight lines." I told him how I had somehow moved east as I walked south. "I keep thinking how Darby must have felt. If he was lost in the woods, he would try to get back to where he started. But he got turned around and instead of going south, he bore east."

"Or north or west," Jack put in.

"OK, OK. But my point is, he keeps going, trying to get back to this house where he knows his mother is waiting for him. Finally, after a very long walk, he sees a house and assumes it's the one he's looking for. Maybe he doesn't even remember what the original house looked like. I don't know how familiar he was with it. He sees a house, knocks on a door, and asks for his mother."

"And somebody takes him in."

"Somebody takes him in," I echoed, trying to think this through.

"And now you've interviewed all or most of the players. Which one was most likely to have done that?"

"Many of them would have taken him in, Jack. Many of the men in the families I've talked to helped in the search. I had a sense of a lot of good people trying to do the right thing."

"But your theory is that the person who took him in did the wrong thing."

"And the question is why." I looked down at the map I had spread out in front of us. The houses on the east, the ones Betty and I had visited together on Monday, were the closest houses to the house Darby had been visiting, which is why we went there first. That didn't necessarily mean he would have found them first. If he had circled left instead of right, west instead of east, he could have come out at the ones I had canvassed today. It would have taken him longer to get there, but as Jack had said, he had to reach a house eventually unless he kept going in circles forever. And if he had been going in circles, the search party might have found him.

"But the answer is obvious," I said. "Because that person who took him in had Larry Filmore in the house and he saw an opportunity to use both those people to his advantage."

"I disagree with you. Darby was lost on a weekday. Filmore left home early on Sunday. I think things happened in reverse. It's even possible Darby came out on a road that Sunday morning and Filmore picked him up."

One of my theories. "And took him wherever he was going, intending to call the police when he got there."

"Sure. Wouldn't you do the same thing?"

"That would mean he walked north to the highway and missed the houses altogether."

"Don't give up your original idea. You haven't disproved anything yet."

"You know what, Jack? Maybe the fact that Larry Filmore and Darby Maxwell came together wasn't a coincidence."

"How's that?"

"Listen." I was feeling excited, as though something reasonable had finally emerged from the morass. "Darby gets lost in the woods. He ends up at somebody's house. The somebody takes him in, maybe because he doesn't have much choice. Here's this young fellow, cold and hungry and dirty, at his doorstep. He gives Darby something to eat and finds out who his mother is and what happened. This person then locks Darby up in the house—"

"Or barn or caretaker's cottage," Jack said.

"Right. Because he thinks he can play this for money. He hears something on the radio or TV and goes into town, where he finds flyers on all the poles. He calls Betty Linton and asks if there's a reward for Darby's return. She says there isn't, or whatever she said. The guy thinks, 'Maybe if I hang on to him, the mother'll pay to get him back.' But there's never any mention of a reward and he doesn't want to get involved in asking for a ransom."

"Because he knows he's likely to be caught picking up the money."

"Exactly. And then it occurs to him. Maybe if he calls Larry Filmore, about whom he knows something threatening, maybe if Filmore comes out, he can work a deal.

Filmore is a philanthropist. He has a reputation for good
works. Maybe he'll come across with more money in return for Darby's life."

"I like it," Jack said. "Let me get this straight. Darby
may have found this house the first night he's lost. The guy
who takes him in sees an opportunity to make a quick buck
and calls Darby's mother. It doesn't work. So he thinks
he'll call Filmore, who may have paid off some blackmail
once, and maybe he'll get Filmore to cough up some more
money to save Darby's life."

"That's it," I said. "What do you think?"

"I think it's a great theory. That would account for why
Darby disappeared for such a long time. It was about a
week, wasn't it?"

"About that," I said. "And he lets them go separately so
no one will put them together."

"You said 'lets them go.' You think he let Larry Filmore
go and he killed himself because he didn't manage to save
Darby? That doesn't figure."

"No, it doesn't. He would have gone right to the police."

"And let the kidnapper spill the beans on his secret?"

"I don't know. This is a tough one."

"They're all tough till you figure them out. I think
you've really got a good scenario there."

"Either Larry was so torn up because saving Darby meant
giving up his secret that he felt he had to kill himself or—"

"I'm listening."

"Or the kidnapper drove to Oakwood with him, killed
him in the car, and made it look like suicide."

"Why'd he go all the way to Oakwood? Why not kill
him and dump the body somewhere that wasn't Oakwood
and wasn't Connecticut?"

"Larry Filmore's wallet was almost empty when it was
returned to Laura. The kidnapper took whatever big bills
Larry had, probably a few hundred dollars. Laura said he

always had that much money with him. It wasn't enough. He wanted much more. Larry said he had more at home, maybe in a safe."

"So the guy drove to Oakwood with Larry to pick up what he could."

"And there wasn't any money and the guy got mad and killed him." I said it quickly, feeling it was what had happened.

"Where did they look for money in the middle of the night? Don't you think Laura would have woken up if she heard someone come into her bedroom? And didn't she tell you her sister-in-law was in the house with her?"

"Maybe they went into the basement," I suggested.

"Maybe." He didn't sound very certain. "They go into the house together, down to the basement where there's supposed to be a safe or something, and then they go back out to the garage and the guy gets Filmore to sit behind the wheel again?"

It didn't sound very smooth. "Well, I don't have all the details worked out."

Jack gave me a grin and leaned over and kissed me. "You're doing better than anyone else. And you're right. It explains why the guy in Connecticut suddenly called Filmore."

"And then called again in the middle of the night. He was anxious, Jack. He wanted to get this done. Filmore rebuffed him when he called during the birthday party. That got him mad. He didn't want to wait another day, so he called in the middle of the night. He wanted to worry Filmore, make him act. I really like this."

"I can see you do. And you're right. It explains the two calls. It explains why Filmore and Darby were in the same place for a while. And the reason why he may have waited a couple of days to finish off Filmore is that he was hoping a reward would be posted for Darby. Then he could return Darby, collect his money, and decide what to do with Filmore."

"He couldn't let him go," I said sadly. "He couldn't be sure Filmore would be quiet about Darby. Filmore was a dead man when that call came in to the church during the party. From that moment, he had only a few days to live."

16

I called Betty Linton first. I asked her to find out what she could about the Pasternaks. I knew it was very tenuous, but Betty recalled that the people living on both sides of the Pasternaks responded guardedly when I asked about them. I know that children make up stories about people in "haunted houses" and maybe this was the same kind of thing, but sometimes the children were right, and maybe these were people who were not being judged unfairly. I remembered how Eddie had held my hand tightly as we stood in the foyer talking to Mrs. Pasternak on Tuesday. I also reminded myself that she had smiled and been nice to him just as we were leaving.

Then I called Laura.

"I'm glad you called," she said. She sounded a little tired.

"Is something up?"

"Tell me why you called."

"A couple of questions. Do you know where Charlie Calhoun lives?"

"Charlie the night watchman?"

"Yes."

"Give me a minute. I'm sure it's on Larry's Rolodex." She moved from wherever she was and I could hear her put the phone down and flip through something. "Here it is, Calhoun. He lives in Connecticut."

"Connecticut! Why didn't you tell me?"

"Chris, I'm sure it was in the back of my mind, but it doesn't matter. Charlie is a good man. He was working the night of the party. Not everyone who lives in Connecticut is under suspicion. He lives nowhere near where Betty Linton lives, believe me."

"Give me the address anyway. I think I'll check it out." I wrote down what she dictated, aware that she was right. It was a long drive from that part of Connecticut to where Darby had been lost. "OK. Second, did your husband keep money hidden in the house?"

There was no answer for several seconds. "I don't think so," she said. "We once talked about the danger of leaving cash around. It's the thing that gets stolen first if you have a break-in. Not that we ever did."

"What I had in mind was a safe," I said.

"We never had one. I have some special pieces of jewelry that I keep in the bank vault until I want to wear them. Then I take them out and return them the first day afterward that the bank is open."

A thought struck me. "Did you take one of those pieces out for the birthday party?"

"I did. A diamond necklace. I notified the insurance company before I took it out, as I always do. They charge insurance for the days it's out of the box."

That was a new one on me, but I don't think I own anything worth more than three figures. She was obviously talking about a lot of zeros in her number. "Was it still in your house after your husband's death?"

"Yes, it was. I didn't get it back for quite some time and I remember getting a huge bill from the insurance company after I returned it and called them to say it was back in the bank."

"OK," I said. "No home safe, no money lying around, one piece of expensive jewelry intact."

"Where are you going with this?" Laura asked.

"I have a theory. It's not exactly destroyed now, but it's a little harder to believe. You said you had something to tell me."

"I found Larry's gun."

"You did? Where?"

She let her breath out. "I took the whole day today to look for it. I went through every one of Larry's drawers. There isn't much in them anymore, because I gave away most of his clothing many years ago, and I didn't expect a gun to turn up there. I went through his closet, which is also pretty empty of his things, but there were boxes of papers on the floor and on a couple of shelves. I went through places I couldn't imagine him ever hiding a gun or anything else, like the hutch cabinet in the dining room where I keep dishes and crystal. I even went down to the basement."

That interested me, because I had suggested Larry Filmore might keep a safe down there. "And you found it," I said.

"No, I didn't. I hauled up a lot of stuff to throw away and give away, but I didn't find the gun. I found it by accident. I took some boxes out to the garage to hold until the garbage is collected, and while I was out there I looked at some things on the side of the garage where Larry kept his car. I noticed that his tackle box was there, locked with a padlock."

"Tackle box?" I asked, thinking of football.

"He was a fisherman. He kept his flies and whatever else in the box and always kept it locked. I never bothered to ask him why. I found the key on the key ring the police gave back to me after he died. It had the house key, the car keys, a bunch of keys for the plant, and a key that matched the padlock. The gun was in the box."

"In a locked box in the garage," I said more to myself

than to her. "That fits with my theory. Have you turned it over to the police?"

"Why should I? He didn't kill himself with it and he didn't use it for anything else, as far as I know. It's licensed, or it was when he died."

"I don't think it's licensed anymore, Laura. You have to keep renewing the license, on your birthday, I think. That would be your husband's birthday, since he was the owner."

"I'll bring it in tomorrow."

"Did you handle it?" I asked.

"I didn't touch it. I saw it and I closed the box up and locked it. It's been there for twelve years, that I'm sure of. Nothing's going to happen to it. You and I are the only two people in the world who know it exists and where it is."

"Thanks for telling me, Laura. When you take it in, why don't you carry in the whole box so the police can take it out without leaving any prints on it."

"What do you expect to find on it?"

"I don't know. Probably nothing except your husband's prints. But who knows? This is a very strange case. If someone else's prints are on it, it may give us a clue to what happened."

"I'll do as you suggest. I'd better go now. I'm exhausted."

Laura called the next morning after she took the tackle box to the police station. The police removed the gun, quite carefully according to her description, and kept the tackle box and whatever else was in it. Since it was Saturday, I didn't expect to hear anything about prints till next week.

Late in the afternoon, Betty called. "I have some information on the Pasternaks," she said.

"You must have worked hard."

"I just got on the phone and called everyone I knew,

which wasn't terribly successful. Then I called the families we talked to a few days ago, starting with Mrs. Farragut. Remember her?"

"Yes, I do. She was friendly and talkative."

"That's the one. It took a little prompting, but she finally said they were a couple that had lived there a pretty long time and they weren't very friendly. There were always arguments with the people next door on the far side and also with her and her husband."

"What kind of arguments?"

"Oh, neighbor things. They leave trash outside and it attracts animals. When you say something to them, they're rude. Their alarm system went off once in the morning and the police couldn't locate them till afternoon to get permission to have someone turn it off. Mrs. Farragut said she nearly died from the sound."

"I can imagine," I said. "I've heard those things from a distance, and they're very annoying."

"It sounded like they keep to themselves and want to live their own way, even if it infringes on other people."

"So there's nothing sinister about them. They're just annoying."

"To put it in a nutshell, yes. Mrs. Farragut said they've been known to dump garbage in the woods, to leave equipment outside for months, creating an eyesore. Generally sloppy. Can you tell me why you asked about them in particular?"

I explained, both how I had spoken to Mrs. Pasternak and how I had stumbled into their backyard yesterday.

"And you think that's where Darby was?"

"Not really. It's just a possibility. Being annoying and sloppy don't add up to kidnapping. I just wanted to check them out."

"Maybe I'll drive over myself and try to talk to them."

"All right."

"And I'll let you know if anything happens."

What happened was that Sister Joseph called early in the evening. It was several weeks since we had spoken, and I was delighted to hear her voice.

"I just looked at my calendar, Chris. I see your son is having a birthday soon."

"That's right. He'll be four."

"Four years. I just can't believe it."

"He'll be in kindergarten in September. It's almost a year away, but these years seem to fly by."

"They certainly do. I hope you'll bring him up here for everyone to see."

"Definitely."

"And there's something else on my calendar. I'm attending a small conference next week in New York."

"Will I get to see you?"

"I hope so. They've scheduled a two-hour lunch on Monday and I thought it would be a good time for me to take you to lunch and have a good talk."

"I won't let you take me, Joseph, but I will certainly come in to see you."

"Do you think Arnold might be available? I haven't seen him in a long time and talking to him is so stimulating."

Arnold Gold, my good friend, sometime employer, fiery lawyer, and defender of all good causes, has an office in downtown Manhattan. "I'll call him and see if he's free."

"Wonderful. Let me know and I'll make a reservation."

Happily, Arnold had no appointments and no court date for Monday and he was as delighted as I at the prospect of seeing Joseph again. When they first met, at our wedding, which took place at St. Stephen's, I thought they were the least likely two people to get along with each other. I have never discussed religion with Arnold and I don't honestly know what he believes, if anything, but he found Joseph as interesting as I find her and she, in turn, was quite fascinated by him. They haven't met often, but each gives me regards for the other regularly.

For me it was a wonderful opportunity to discuss the case with both of them. On Sunday, when I had a little free time in the afternoon, I organized both my notes and my thoughts so I would be ready for the challenge.

"Want to take a quick ride up to where this guy Charlie Calhoun lives?" Jack asked as I pushed my papers around.

"I wouldn't mind."

"It's not that far. We don't have to stop and talk, just look at the house, see if there's a barn out back—"

"If it's just Charlie and his wife, they could be in on it together," I said. "Charlie could have called from the plant and his wife could have been waiting for Filmore at the house."

"Let's take a look."

The three of us got in the car and drove off. When we got to the Calhoun house, I felt a little ashamed. It was so far from where Darby got lost that it would have taken Darby a couple of days of walking to get there, and the likelihood that he would not have stopped and asked for help long before that was very slim.

The house was not in one of those classy rustic areas where houses sat on acres of land. It was a small house with one very similar to it on either side, a short driveway, and a one-car garage.

"Well, I tried," I said.

"You can't leave loose ends. From what you told me about him, I'm glad he's not a suspect."

"Me, too."

Jack drove to the end of the street, made a U-turn, and started back.

"I want ice cream," a voice from the backseat said.

"Ice cream!" Jack said. "What's that?"

"You know what ice cream is, Daddy."

"OK, kiddo. I guess if we take a drive on Sunday, we know how it'll end up."

It ended up a little drippy, but we all enjoyed it.

17

I don't go into New York all that often, and it's frequently a mixed experience. Depending on when you go, the traffic may be fairly light or so heavy you wish you hadn't started out. The worst thing about it is parking. When I was newly released from my vows and I drove into the city for the first time, alone at the wheel, I was stunned at the cost of parking. That was about six years ago and it has gotten worse. Jack tells me not to worry about it, that I do it so seldom that it doesn't make a difference, but paying over twenty dollars for the privilege of getting out of my car and getting somewhere on foot still gives me palpitations.

There had been some back-and-forth between Joseph and me, and between Arnold and me, everybody arguing about where to eat and each one insisting on paying. I had made up my mind to pick up the bill myself and pay with my one credit card, courtesy of my husband, who insisted I carry it. The restaurant was far enough east that I was able to park at a lower rate. One of the things you learn as an out-of-town driver is that the closer you are to Fifth Avenue, the spiritual and financial main artery of the city, the more it costs to park. Get over to a river and the rates come down substantially.

I got to the restaurant at exactly twelve-fifteen and found that Arnold was already there. We hugged and kissed and he asked to see the latest pictures of Eddie, and just as he finished with the last one Joseph arrived.

Joseph is a tall woman with a face I find absolutely beautiful. Although we have known each other for about twenty years, I see no change in her face or her body. Her skin is as clear and unblemished as the day I first laid eyes on her, her eyes, through the glasses she always wears, as bright and intelligent as ever. She walks with purpose. I cannot imagine her dawdling anywhere, although our walks together on the campus at St. Stephen's are somewhat lackadaisical.

As she saw us, she brightened and smiled, hurried to the table, and greeted us with obvious pleasure.

"Arnold, I am so glad to see you," she said after hugging me. "It's been a very long time and my brain needs some stimulation."

He was out of his seat to help her into hers. "Good to see you, Sister. Let me put your briefcase on the empty chair."

"Thank you. I should have left it behind. It got heavier as I walked."

"How about a drink?" Arnold said. "It's a cold day out there."

I had a glass of sherry while my two friends had Scotch. We toasted our health and talked so long the waiter got tired of waiting for our order. Finally, Joseph remembered she had a meeting in the afternoon and we turned our attention to the food.

Joseph took Arnold's advice and ordered what he did. I am still somewhat hesitant about food I'm not familiar with, so I ordered the tuna fish and asked to have it well done. I've noticed that people in the know now request their tuna rare in the middle. I have a long way to go.

"Still eating tuna for lunch?" Arnold teased.

"This isn't out of a can. It's not the same thing."

Arnold kept an obvious riposte to himself.

"Well, I'm just delighted to be with you both at the same time," Joseph said. "Oakwood must have become a safe place to live. I haven't gotten a call from you since last spring, Chris."

"Oh, dear," I said.

"You're not involved in another one." Joseph sounded almost incredulous.

"And I have the good fortune to be present at the famous sessions in which Chrissie lays it on the table and Sister Joseph pulls a killer out of the hat."

"Not this time," I said.

"I've never pulled a killer out of anywhere, Arnold," Joseph said. "I play the part of a hunting dog. I point."

"Well, let's hear it."

I took my notebook out of my bag, flipped to the page marked *Darby Maxwell*, and started to tell them what I had found in Aunt Margaret's boxes in the basement. I went on to talk about Celia Yaeger, the former mayor's wife who knew everyone and everything and who led me to Laura Filmore after I had spoken to Virginia at Greenwillow about Darby. I went on and on, my first meeting with Betty, our dinner with Laura.

"Let me get this straight," Arnold said. He had an intense look on his face. A few minutes into my narrative he had taken an envelope out of his pocket and begun to take notes while Joseph pulled a few sheets of white paper out of her briefcase and started to do the same. "You discovered that two people who met with unusual deaths in two different places, people who never knew each other, were wearing each other's sneakers when they were found dead."

"Yes," I said.

"That's incredible. No one noticed before that these men were wearing the wrong shoes?"

"Each of the men's survivors noticed it, but it was after

the men were buried. Each survivor called the medical examiner's office in her area and made inquiries."

"And no one ever put it together till you did."

"No one could," I said. "One body was in Oakwood,
New York, and the other was in Connecticut. One survivor
lives in Oakwood and the other in Connecticut. They never
knew each other. It was just because my aunt attended both
funerals and knew both victims that I happened to put it
together."

I went on, detailing my visits to Connecticut, my theories about what had happened, and the scenario I had
worked out over the weekend. "I guess that's it," I said,
coming to the end of the last page of handwriting.

"You believe that the two victims were together in the
same house for a period of time shortly before their
deaths," Joseph said.

"Yes."

"And you don't think it was an accident that they were
together. You think the person you call the blackmailer
found Darby Maxwell, or Darby found him while wan-
dering in the woods, and the blackmailer saw an opportunity to make money."

"That's what I think. At the beginning, I thought the two
men came together accidentally, but I don't believe that
anymore."

"Interesting," Arnold said. "More than interesting. So
you've got to find this blackmailer and you're looking for
him from two different directions, through Laura Filmore
and by talking to the people who live in the area Darby got
lost in."

"Right. And neither journey has been very productive.
All the people who were living there twelve years ago remember what happened. Several of the men took part in
the search party. No one admits to having seen him."

"You didn't really expect they would, did you?" Arnold is nothing if not a realist.

"I didn't expect anyone to answer 'yes' to the question, but I've asked each person if he knew Larry Filmore. I've watched their faces as I said the name. None of them gave the slightest indication it was a familiar name."

"There seem to be no suspects," Joseph said. "Except for Charlie Calhoun, the night watchman, and I agree that's pretty farfetched."

"There aren't any suspects because Chris doesn't know enough yet. I'll tell you what I think. You're right that Filmore had some kind of secret he was protecting. But his wife knew about it. She knows. She's still protecting it."

"I'm afraid I have to agree," Joseph said, "at least in part."

"Do you think she knew where her husband went?" I asked. "I know I've lost my objectivity, but I really believe she loved him. And as my friend Mel pointed out, she didn't run off with another man or spend a million dollars after he died. She's lived quietly; she's volunteered for good causes. I like her very much."

"And because she's that kind of person, she wants to keep what she knows to herself."

"What could he have done?" I asked.

"He could have killed someone in a fight," Arnold said. "These things happen. Someone stops you on the street, demands money, and you punch him out. He knocks his head on a building and you walk away and get in your car, but someone sees your license plate. Or he could have cooked the books in his company so he made a fortune and the stockholders were swindled. People have killed themselves for less."

"Let me ask you something," Joseph said. "Do you have any reason to believe that Larry Filmore was responsible for Darby's death?"

"No, I don't. Darby was left to die in the woods on a cold night. My feeling is the blackmailer thought Darby was no longer useful to him. He knew by then that Darby was retarded. If Darby was found alive and told a strange story of being in someone's house, it might be discounted because of his mental abilities."

"His mother would know what to believe," Joseph said.

"I'm sure she would, but would *she* be believed? And we're not talking about reality; we're talking about what this blackmailer thought. When Larry Filmore got to Connecticut and refused to go along with his demands, it was time to get rid of both of them. Larry had to die because he could tell the police that Darby was being held against his will. Darby could be let go because there was a fair chance he wouldn't survive and if he did, he would be considered incoherent if he told a wild story."

"I think I agree with you on that."

"So do I," Arnold said. "The question is, how do we find this person?"

"That's my question."

"You have to press Laura Filmore," Arnold said. "She has to tell you what it is her husband did and you work from that."

"But suppose," I said, "that your first hypothesis is the right one, that Filmore accidentally killed a man who was trying to rob him on the street, maybe here in New York. A potential Good Samaritan is standing in the shadows or walks by across the street. Filmore dashes to his car, turns on the motor and the lights, and the observer writes down the license plate number."

"Which he should take to the police but doesn't," Arnold said.

"He looks at the car. It's big and expensive. Somehow he finds out what Filmore's address is. Maybe he even drives up to Oakwood and looks at the house. It's a very impressive house, Arnold. I'm sure it's worth a million dollars or more."

Arnold grinned. "And if you think it's worth a million, it's probably worth two."

"Not out of the question," I agreed. What things cost never fails to amaze me. "The observer decides he'd rather get Filmore to pay him to keep quiet than go to the police and report what he saw."

"So far, so good. And this observer, as you call him, may live in Connecticut. He may have been in the city for dinner and the theater as Filmore probably was. So he starts to hound Filmore for money."

"I'm not sure I agree with you," Joseph said.

Arnold bowed his head deferentially. "Please. I'd like to hear what you think."

"You and I seem to agree that Laura knew about the threats. But Chris is convinced, and I'm willing to go with her assessment, that Laura loved her husband."

"OK," Arnold said. "Where does that lead us?"

"To the question of why she didn't tell the police her husband was in Connecticut. When he didn't return on Sunday, she must have suspected that something terrible was happening. She called the police because she feared for his life. Why at that point would she refuse to tell the police where he'd gone?"

"Because she didn't know."

"That's my point. The person who witnessed the incident we've dreamed up didn't live in Connecticut."

"Then we're in big trouble," Arnold said. "If he didn't live in Connecticut, he could be anywhere in the world. We have nothing to go on."

"But he was living there at the time of the birthday party," Joseph said. "He wasn't a Connecticut home owner; he was a visitor, a . . ." She tried to find the right word.

"A caretaker," I said. "Someone who lived in a cottage behind a house."

"Exactly. We don't know when he started delivering threats to Larry Filmore. His wife probably does and she isn't talking. But if the incident happened some time before Filmore's birthday—months or even years before— the observer may have lived in New York or wherever the incident happened. Or he may have been a visitor. But at the time of the great birthday party, he was in Connecticut, a place he may never have been before when he contacted Filmore in the past."

"I see why you turn to Sister Joseph," Arnold said. "What you're telling us is that maybe twenty years ago Filmore had an incident. After he was contacted by the observer, he may have sent money to a box number somewhere."

"Yes, to a place that had nothing to do with where the Filmores live or where the incident happened."

"But the observer always knows where Filmore lives. And when Darby Maxwell gets lost in the Connecticut woods, the observer is living there. Maybe he's some-body's caretaker; maybe he's renting a cottage for a while. Or maybe he's a house sitter. They do that, you know. People want to make sure the heat goes on and the house looks lived in. They might not even be charging rent for the place."

"There is one family that was away when Darby was lost," I said. "I remember them. Betty and I talked to them the first day."

"Then that's a possibility," Joseph said. "You should certainly go back and talk to them again."

"They didn't mention a house sitter." I wrote myself a reminder anyway. Somehow, I didn't think of the Gal-laghers as people who would get a house sitter, but I hardly knew them. It was worth a try. "But why didn't Larry tell his wife where he was going?"

"He didn't want to upset her," Arnold said. "It was the middle of the night. They'd had a big party. He thought he'd go up there, do his business, and get back in a few hours. He didn't expect to be held hostage."

"There could be another reason," Joseph said. We looked at her. "Maybe Mr. Filmore wasn't the one who had the incident."

"What makes you say that?" I asked.

"I'm thinking of the relationship between the husband and wife. If he had the incident, especially if she was present when it happened, he might just have brushed it off casually so that she wouldn't worry. If the observer called with a demand, he might say, 'I'll take care of it; don't give it a thought.' But suppose one of their children was involved in an incident."

"They're kind of young for that; at least, they were twelve years ago," I said. "They were probably teenagers."

Arnold laughed. "You think teenagers don't get in trouble?"

"OK. I'll follow up on it."

"Or," Joseph went on, "Mrs. Filmore could have been involved in an incident herself."

"I suppose so." I could hear the skepticism in my voice.

"And in those cases, she might well want to know exactly what was going on and he might try his best to protect her from the truth."

I tried to think how Jack and I would handle such a thing, but there was no comparison. Jack would go to the police, no matter how difficult it was. And so would I, or so I wanted to believe. Eddie is much too young for the kind of mischief we were talking about. "So he told her it was trouble at the plant so she wouldn't know the blackmailer of her child or herself was back."

"I think that's reasonable."

"Have you both given up the idea that the husband is the one who had the incident?" Arnold asked.

Joseph laughed. "I haven't given up any ideas; I just think we have to consider all possible alternatives."

"Mrs. Filmore isn't likely to have killed someone in the street after he attacked her."

"No, but there are other ways of killing someone."

"True."

"I don't look forward to this conversation," I said. "But I will do it. And I'll check on the Gallaghers in Connecticut."

"I think we should all have dessert," Arnold said. "We've used up a lot of energy in the last hour, and some sweets might replace some of that."

So we looked at the dessert menu and selected wonderful-sounding treats. I knew I wouldn't eat anything else till to-morrow morning, so why not enjoy this meal even more?

"How was the tuna?" Arnold asked.

"Much better than in a can."

"Glad to hear it."

"I'll have to dash as soon as I've had dessert," Joseph said. "I'm afraid I'll be a little late as it is."

"I'll get you there in a taxi," Arnold said gallantly.

"Oh, Arnold, that's really unnecessary. And a walk will do me good."

Arnold waved away her offer. Then he said, "This is a very interesting case, especially considering it started with a mix-up of sneakers. You know, Chrissie, we may all be wrong about all of this."

"I know, but when explanations sound possible and rea-sonable I think they're worth following up."

We dropped the case and talked about ourselves as we ate sweets and drank coffee. I noticed that Arnold was dressed much more elegantly than usual. When he's not in court, he tends toward the open shirt, the knot of the tie pulled down, sleeves rolled if he's sitting at his desk. Today he looked like a lawyer, his lanky frame in a dark suit, crisp white shirt, and dark tie with a subtle pattern. Even his hair looked tamed. Joseph, of course, wore the brown habit of Franciscan nuns, her skirt about midcalf, her shoes sensible, her bag black, large and old enough to show wear. As I looked at it, I knew what I would give her for Christmas, and I was happy to have thought of something she would use daily.

As Joseph asked for the bill, the waiter told her "the gentleman" had taken care of it. That was why he was the first one there. We left in something of a hurry, Joseph concerned that she would be missed at the afternoon meeting. A taxi came by almost immediately, its light on, and Arnold flagged it down. I wished them both a quick good-bye and went to ransom my car.

18

As I walked to my garage, I looked at the street I was on, the doorways, the signs prohibiting parking till seven at night, the garbage bags in large bunches near the curb awaiting pickup. Arnold's scenario of the Incident—I thought of it with a capital *I*—was very plausible. Once you got out of the theater district or stayed off the north–south avenues, the streets, which went east and west, might well be dark and empty, especially as you left the center of the city. I remembered a time when Jack and I had gone into New York and found a parking place on the street, thrilled that we would save a small fortune, and an unsavory-looking man had bothered us as we walked back to our car. If it had happened to us, it could have happened to anyone. Jack told him to get on his way and he did, but the memory, the chill of fear, had remained with me for a long time.

I went down into my garage, feeling safe, paid for my car, and drove home.

"Laura, I think we have to talk." I had picked up Eddie and gone home, and now I was talking to Laura Filmore on the phone.

"Sure. Would you like to come over?"

I looked at my watch. I had some leftovers I would reheat for Jack and Eddie, and that wouldn't take long. "May I bring my son?"

"Of course. I'm just reading the paper, so you won't be interrupting."

I drove over, left my car in the driveway, and took Eddie to the front door. Laura answered my ring and welcomed Eddie.

"We came to this house before," he said, looking around.

Laura laughed. "Yes, you did, Eddie. You can play in the playroom again. There are lots of toys there."

"Our house has lots of toys, too. But your house is bigger."

"Do you like big houses?"

Eddie nodded several times. "I like this house."

Coffee was dripping in the kitchen, and Laura took a tray to the room we had sat in before. Eddie found things to play with in the adjoining room, and Laura and I sat and sipped. I turned down cake because I couldn't even think about eating anything else, but my dependable son was happy to eat my share as well as his.

"Laura, I've just spent an hour or so with two friends of mine and we talked about this case."

"Were they helpful?"

"They dreamed up some possible explanations for why your husband took off that night. What's interesting is that my friends felt sure you knew your husband was paying someone off and why he was doing that."

"Why would they think that?" she asked.

"It seemed to fit the facts. Did you know where your husband went the night of the party?"

"Chris, if I had known, I would have told the police. The last thing I wanted was for Larry to end up dead. He told me he was going to the plant. It wasn't the first time he'd been woken up by a problem there."

"Did you and Larry drive into New York a lot?"

"Fairly frequently. We went to the theater; we went to Lincoln Center. We had friends there who invited us for the evening."

"Did you drive in on those occasions?"

"Yes."

"And where did you park?"

"In whatever garage was nearby."

"Did you ever park on the street?"

"Never. Larry drove an expensive car. He was afraid it would be damaged or stolen. New York streets aren't that safe for big, expensive cars. We always went to a garage."

But even if you parked in a garage, I thought, you had to walk to it. Someone might have approached them as they neared their garage, and the observer could have waited till they drove out of the garage to see the license plate. But I didn't want to ask her point-blank about the Incident.

"Why are you asking these questions?" she asked when I didn't say anything.

"Just an idea I had. I believe you didn't know where your husband went when he got up in the middle of the night. But I think you know what I'm trying to find out."

"I don't. I don't think anyone was blackmailing him. I don't know any reason why anyone would. He lived a clean, pure life."

"Someone called him at the party. Someone called him in the middle of the night after his birthday."

"I don't know who it was. I don't know where the call came from."

"You know what it was about," I said, looking her straight in the eye.

"I think maybe this has gone too far. You haven't learned anything useful and you're making things up. I think it's gotten to you, Chris. You should forget it. I want so much to know why my husband died and whether someone was involved in his suicide, but I don't want to make myself crazy."

"Laura, whatever it was, your husband is beyond being embarrassed by it."

"There was nothing to embarrass him, Chris, nothing. You've gotten a bug in your head; you're telling people a fictional story that's one-sided. . . . Larry didn't do anything. I'm telling you the truth." She was agitated now and looked distressed.

I knew I had handled this badly, but I didn't know how else to do it. Should I have tried to contact all the surviving people who had been at the birthday party and question them? What could I have done differently? If this woman was the only living person—besides the blackmailer or observer that we had hypothesized—all she had to do was keep quiet and no one would ever know the truth. There was certainly a great advantage in not confiding a secret to anyone.

"Was it you then?" I asked.

"Was what me?"

"The person who was being blackmailed?"

"No one in my family was being blackmailed."

"Then why did your husband get a call—two calls—the night of the party? And why did he drive to Connecticut?"

"I don't know. I don't know." There was a sound of desperation in her voice. Then she said, "This has to end. Please, let this be. Whatever happened that night, whatever happened those days after the party, we're never going to find out, and I don't think I can take this anymore."

"I'm sorry, Laura. I didn't know when I started that this would happen. I don't want to cause you such anguish. I may be wrong about the blackmail, but you and I both know that something happened twelve years ago or more and your husband left the house to try to cope with it.

Think about it, OK? Two lives were lost and I'm sure the same person is responsible, directly or indirectly, for what happened."

I got up and flipped my notebook closed. "Come on, Eddie. We have to get home."

"I don't wanna go. I wanna stay here."

"We can't stay here. Daddy's coming home soon and I've got to get dinner ready."

"Please?"

"You can come another time, Eddie," Laura said with a smile, as though none of the words between us had been uttered.

"OK. I'm coming tomorrow."

Laura picked up the tray and I took Eddie's glass and we walked back to the kitchen. On the counter were several bright orange fruits that I had seen before but had never tasted. "What are those?" I asked.

"Persimmons. Haven't you ever eaten one?"

"No. What are they like?"

Laura laughed. "Like heaven on earth. Here, take one." She gave me a large one, stem side down, pointed end up. "Put it on your counter for a another few days. It needs to be just a little riper. I look forward to fall because I love them so much. We used to pick them off the tree when I was a kid."

"Thank you very much. How do you eat them?"

"I'm ashamed to say it, but I just pull a little skin off the pointed end here and go to it. It's best if you're leaning over the sink. If you're too polite to do it that way, you can peel it back and use a small spoon. Here. Let me give you a plastic bag."

"This is fine. Thank you. I'll let you know how I like it."

Eddie carried it like a prize as we drove home, and I put it on the counter as Laura had suggested. I looked forward to enjoying my treat at the end of the week.

* * *

I took myself back to Connecticut the next day. Jack and I had talked at length Monday night, about both of my conversations. I told him I had reached a dead end with Laura. Whoever she was protecting—her husband, herself, her children—unless I came up with something new and convincing, she was unlikely to give an inch. But what could I come up with?

I pulled into the Gallaghers' driveway and went up to the front door.

Mrs. Gallagher answered the bell and invited me in. "Hi. I remember you. It's about the boy who was lost in the woods."

"Right. And you were away when it happened."

"Definitely. Come into the kitchen. We can sit. My husband's in his office, pretending to work."

I looked at her questioningly.

"I'm just kidding. He's at a hard place and he's trying to get some results on that computer of his. I just tease him a little."

We sat down at her kitchen table. Outside the window I could see the backyard and the woods, the trees all bare. It was very pretty and I could imagine how much more beautiful it would be in the spring and summer.

"Mrs. Gallagher, when you and your husband go away, do you ever get anyone to stay in your house?"

"While we're gone?"

"Yes."

"No. We just lock up and go. We have lights on timers, but the truth is, I don't think anyone drives down this road looking to break in. We've lived here a long time and it's very safe."

"You've never had a house sitter?"

"Uh-uh. Why do you ask?"

"Somebody around here must have taken Darby Maxwell in. I thought if you had someone living here while you were gone—"

"Oh, I see. No. Like I said, we lock up tight and we go. I don't even keep plants in the house because we travel a few times a year and I don't want to have to ask anyone to water them. My plants are all outside." She waved toward the window. "Nature takes care of them for me."

Her husband walked into the kitchen just then. "Miss Bennett," he said. "Good morning."

"Good morning, Mr. Gallagher. I was just asking your wife a couple of questions."

"Anything I can help with?"

"She wanted to know if we left someone in the house when we went on vacation," his wife said.

"Nah," he said. "We put the heat down to fifty-five so the pipes don't freeze and we take off. We've never had any trouble. Michelle next-door keeps her eye open. If she sees any funny stuff, she calls the police."

"Has that ever happened?"

"There was a power outage once and the timers all went crazy. The lights were going on during the day and they were off all night. We left a key with the police and she called and they came out and reset everything."

"I see."

"You don't look happy," he said.

"I just don't seem to be making progress."

"Oh, gosh," Mrs. Gallagher said. "You're so down. Things'll turn up. They always do."

"Even for me," her husband said. "I spend my time working on unsolvable problems, so I know how you feel."

"And you solve them?"

"Most of the time. If I didn't, I wouldn't get paid. It's a matter of looking at the problem from different points of view."

"Thanks," I said. "I appreciate your help and your encouragement."

I went outside and got in the car. How many points of view could there be? I had one; Jack had one; Joseph and Arnold had contributed theirs. I was convinced that what Jack and I had worked out the other night was right, that Darby had stumbled into one of these houses and, by coincidence, the blackmailer of Lawrence Filmore took him in and saw an opportunity to make money. But I couldn't go any further unless Laura told me what I was sure she knew.

I started the car and drove down the road to the Franklins' house. Michelle Franklin was home and invited me in.

"Still trying to find out what happened to that retarded boy?" she asked as we sat in her kitchen.

"Still trying and not getting anywhere. I was just talking to the Gallaghers. They said once when they were away there was a power outage and you called the police to reset their timers."

"I remember that. We got an awful snowstorm. Couldn't heat the house except with the fireplace. We rounded up our sleeping bags and slept in the living room."

"When was that?" I asked, grasping at straws.

"Three or four years ago."

No good, I thought. "I walked through the woods the other day," I told her.

"That's pretty dangerous if you don't know the terrain."

"I had a compass."

"Good. I'd hate to have to organize a search party for you."

"Do you ever go away and leave a house sitter here?"

"I don't have to. I have my mother next-door."

"Of course."

"Anyone around here have a barn or a cottage out back?"

"Not here, but there's lots of them around."

"I've seen some," I said.

"I remember they thought he might have fallen in the pond," Michelle said. "Did you see the pond?"

"Yes, I did."

"There have been some drownings there, not for a long time, but you don't forget something like that."

"But Darby didn't drown."

"No."

"Well, I guess I'd better get back. I have to send invitations for my son's birthday party. It's coming up pretty soon."

"That's fun." She smiled. "Give me your number. Maybe I'll think of something."

I wrote it down, thinking she was feeling sorry for me. But you never know. People remember things.

After I picked up Eddie, we went to one of our favorite stores and picked out invitations, paper plates, napkins, candles, and party favors. Eddie was very excited about it. I let him do all the choosing and he carried the bag back to the car when we were done. At home, he took everything out to look at each purchase. We talked about where the party would be, where everyone would sit. Then he sat down with me and I wrote out the invitations.

When Jack came home, he had some mysterious packages with him. I knew he wanted to get Eddie a baseball mitt, and from the shape of one package I assumed there was a bat to go with it. I hoped Eddie could be persuaded not to try them out inside the house.

Later Jack told me he had gotten the results of the tests on the gun Laura had found in her garage. "Only Filmore's prints and not many of them. The gun was wrapped in soft silicon cloth to prevent rust from forming. He kept it clean and I'd be willing to bet Laura was telling the truth that she didn't know where it was. It sounded like no one had touched it since Filmore did."

"Did they dust the box?" I asked.

"They did. She brought it in in a shopping bag. They said it was pretty dusty and they couldn't pick up anything useful on it."

"What's going to happen to the gun?"

"Laura turned it in. She said she doesn't want a gun in the house and I doubt whether they'd give her a license for it. It was loaded, by the way."

"It was?"

"Yup. Filmore meant business. I'm glad no one came across it all these years. Could have been a tragedy."

"Well, there we are. I've exhausted every lead and possibility I can think of. The people who were away when Darby was lost left their house locked up with no house sitter. Either one of those very nice people is lying or Darby got himself to a house that's beyond the ones we checked out."

"Or a house that isn't there anymore," Jack said.

"What do you mean?"

"Houses burn down. Sometimes they're razed and a bigger one is built."

"I'll think about it," I said without enthusiasm.

"What's that thing on the kitchen counter?"

"A persimmon. Laura gave it to me yesterday. She said they picked them when she was a child. I've never eaten one. Have you?"

"I'm not sure. It's a pretty color."

"She says they're heavenly, but they need to be very ripe. I'll let you know after I eat it."

19

I had a great class on Wednesday. The students were lively and argumentative. Nobody slept; nobody even yawned. Most of the class had already begun to read the Block book, and a few of them were confused. The book had been made into a movie and, as often happens, changes had been made that were troubling. In the books, the city of New York was almost a character. On-screen, the book took place in Los Angeles.

My students were irate. How could Hollywood do this? The discussion almost went out of control, but they spoke with such passion, with such feeling, that I let it continue. The handful of students who had not yet started the book were almost jealous of those who were already reading it.

When I went down to the cafeteria afterward, several students asked if they might join me for lunch and we continued talking on several related subjects. I felt exhilarated when I was finally in the car driving home.

I had mailed the invitations to Eddie's party late the previous afternoon, and apparently they had arrived, at least the ones sent to Oakwood addresses, in today's mail. There were two messages on my machine from mothers of young guests accepting. I let Eddie listen to the messages so he would know his friends were looking forward to his party.

One of the problems I had was what to serve the children. The memory of food poisoning at Ryan's party was still very fresh and the mystery still unsolved. I decided perhaps pizza was a better idea than hamburgers, especially since I wouldn't be cooking out-of-doors. I could pick up the pies and reheat them one by one. Jack agreed that was a good idea and suggested that for those of us who were past single digits in age we might consider ordering a pie with pepperoni, mushrooms, and anchovies. I promised to do so.

Late that evening, when we were already upstairs and getting ready for bed, the phone rang. Jack picked it up, said a few words, and handed it to me. "Laura Filmore," he said with his hand over the phone.

"Hello?"

"This is Laura." She sounded serious.

"Hi, Laura. Is something wrong?"

"I want to talk to you. Now. Can you come over?"

I looked at my watch. I didn't really want to do anything but go to sleep, but she sounded as though something important had come up. "I'll be there in ten minutes." I hung up and told Jack where I was going.

"I don't want you to go," he said.

I was startled. "Why?"

"I don't like this. Call her back and tell her to come here. Lay it on me. I just don't want you alone with her in her house right now."

It was clear that he was worried. I picked up the phone and dialed Laura's number.

"I'll pick her up and drive her here," Jack said, reaching for his shoes.

"Yes, all right," Laura said finally, sounding reluctant. "I'll drive myself. Jack doesn't have to go out."

"I'll stay up here while you talk," Jack said when I told him she would drive herself.

Feeling nervous, I went downstairs and turned the light on over the front door. I couldn't remember a time Jack had reacted that way. He sometimes expressed reservations at what I did and where I went, but he had never said, "Don't go," before. I didn't like it.

Laura rang the doorbell about ten minutes later. I had the feeling she might have had to dress before leaving the house and maybe that was why she had asked me to join her rather than the other way around. She was wearing jeans, a big smoky blue cashmere sweater with a cowl neckline, and sneakers, no jewelry, and her hair looked as though she hadn't put it in place after she pulled on the sweater. I was struck by what a good-looking woman she was, and I thought again that if she had wanted to remarry after her husband died, she could have found someone easily.

"It's cold out," she said.

"I've got the heat up in the family room. Give me your coat."

"I'll drop it on a chair. I'm not staying long."

We walked through the kitchen and she stopped suddenly. "That's my persimmon. You haven't eaten it yet."

"You said to let it ripen a few days."

She touched it. "Eat it tomorrow. I think it's ready."

We went into the family room and I shut the door between it and the kitchen to keep the heat in.

"Are you all right?" I asked.

"I'm fine. I've been thinking about what we talked about the other afternoon, about what you said."

I tried to remember what I had said to her. It was after my lunch with Joseph and Arnold. They had both believed Laura knew more than she was telling me. "We talked about a lot of things," I hedged.

"I am going to tell you the truth," she said. "And after that, you will understand why I want you to stop this investigation and to forget what I'm about to tell you."

"I'm listening."

"Where is Jack?"

"He's upstairs. He can't hear us."

She got up, opened the door to the kitchen, saw that no one was there, and sat down again. "You're right. I know why someone called my husband."

I almost stopped breathing. "Tell me, Laura."

"It wasn't Larry; it was me."

So Joseph had been right. "OK."

"I was driving on Route Two-eighty-seven one night. There was an accident with another car. I left the scene. That's the story."

"You didn't report it."

"No. And the other driver told the police it was a hit-and-run and he didn't get my license plate."

"Why didn't you go to the police?"

"I couldn't."

"You were drunk," I said.

"I wasn't drunk. I hadn't had a drink for days. There was no alcohol in my system."

"Were you at fault?"

"I don't know who was at fault."

I stopped to think about what she had said. "But he did have your plate number."

"Yes. That's how he got our name. That's how he got our phone number, Larry's number. That's how he came to call Larry and threaten to expose me if we didn't pay up."

I was sure she had rehearsed this. That was why she had waited till late at night before calling. Something of the truth was in this story, but much of what she had said might be false. If I checked on hit-and-run accidents on Route 287, I would never find anything about this one. It had probably happened somewhere else, perhaps not even in New York State.

"When did this happen?" I asked.

"More than twelve years ago. I'm sure you've figured that out already."

"You were able to drive your car home?"

"Mine was less badly damaged."

"Was someone hurt in the accident, Laura?"

She stared in front of her. "I've told you all I'm going to tell. I just want you to stop. My husband died because of this. I live with that knowledge every day of my life."

"Why didn't you just go to the police?" I asked. "Just tell them what happened and that the other driver was blackmailing you?"

"I couldn't."

"Did you kill someone, Laura?" I could hardly bring myself to ask the question.

"I've finished my story. I can't answer any more questions. I just want you to know that when my husband left our house that night after the party, he told me he was going to the plant. I didn't know he had gotten a call earlier in the evening until you showed me that picture. I'm sure you're right that the blackmailer got Larry and Darby Maxwell together and tried to use Darby to get Larry to come up with more money. If I had known where Larry was, I would have told the police regardless of the consequences."

That had the ring of truth. "When the driver of the other car first called your husband, did Larry pay him off?"

"Yes."

"A lot of money?"

"Yes."

"How did he make the payoff? In person? In the mail?"

She closed her eyes. "I don't want to answer these questions, Chris. Larry paid him off. He never went to Connecticut. He just paid him. And paid him again."

"I see."

"And then we thought it was over. But we were wrong."

"That person, the blackmailer, he must have had some

proof that you were at the wheel of the car the night of the accident."

Laura stood and put on her jacket. It was a beautiful warm-looking shearling. "He had a piece of evidence," she admitted. "It was enough to convict me. It was enough to destroy my life."

I got up and opened the door to the kitchen. The kitchen was ice-cold and I shivered.

"Will you stop?" she said. "Will you leave me in peace? I pay for what happened. I pay much more than money. I will never stop paying. Isn't that enough?"

"It is enough," I said. But it wasn't that simple. There was Darby.

We walked through the house to the front door. The light was still on outside.

"Can you drive?" I asked.

"Yes. I can drive. Can you forgive?"

She was down the steps before I could answer.

When her car had gone down to the end of Pine Brook Road, I turned off the light, checked to make sure the door was locked, and went upstairs. Jack was wearing his navy blue terry cloth robe and was propped on the bed reading a book. He closed it and looked up at me as I came into the room.

"Curiouser and curiouser," I said. I sat down and told him what I had just learned.

"Evidence," he said, picking out the crucial word in my story.

"I can't think what it is. I asked her if she was drunk and she said she hadn't had a drink in several days."

"What makes you think she was telling you the truth this time?"

"I don't know for sure. Maybe because she admitted to something that could be a felony. I think she mixed some truth with some fiction so that I couldn't possibly figure out when this accident happened or on what road. She was specific about saying Route Two-eighty-seven, but I think she wanted to put me off. I would guess that it really happened at night, as she said, or there would have been a bunch of cars full of witnesses. But what piece of evidence could the other driver have taken away?"

"A piece of her car, a fender maybe."

"But that car is long gone, maybe twenty years gone, so a fender wouldn't do much good now, but she still won't come clean on the accident. It has to be something else, something tied directly to her."

"Maybe she had the suicide gun with her."

"Mm." I thought about it. "Larry Filmore got the gun illegally and let her take it with her for protection when she drove alone. That would explain why she didn't want the Oakwood Police pursuing the history of that gun beyond Officer Reilly."

"It would have her prints on it," Jack said, "just from putting it in the car."

"Laura's not the kind of person who would carry a gun."

"That remains to be seen. I'm going to check on that suicide gun tomorrow. It's time to get back to basics, investigation one-o-one, read all the reports, don't assume anything. All the information I got on it was secondhand, from the Oakwood Police, and all they told me was that the cop in New York lost it in a snowstorm. Let me see if there's more."

"My feeling is that someone died in that car accident," I said.

"I get the same feeling. That's why she can't own up to it even fifteen or twenty years later."

"But why didn't the survivor in the other car just tell the police what the plate number was?"

"Could be a lot of things. Maybe he'd picked up a hitchhiker and that's who died. The driver didn't give a damn about bringing her to justice. He just saw a chance to make some easy money."

"A crime of opportunity," I said. "Just like what we're speculating happened with Darby. It's how this guy operates." I leaned over and pulled my shoes off. "Let's see if anything interesting turns up on that gun and then I'll try to figure out where to go."

"Why did she run?" Jack said, almost to himself.

"Because she looked in the other car and saw that someone was badly hurt. She panicked."

"You can always make a case that it was the other guy's fault."

"She wasn't thinking straight, Jack. Your car gets hit, you get disoriented."

"But later, when she got home, when she talked to her husband, when she calmed down, what kept her from turning herself in then with a really good lawyer at her side?"

"You think it has to do with the mysterious piece of evidence?"

"I don't know, but I sure as hell want to find out."

I felt the same way, although I defended Laura's actions in my own mind with the arguments I had given to Jack. On Thursday morning, I took Eddie shopping and cleaned up the house when we got back. Several more mothers called about the party, one saying her daughter couldn't make it. That still left us with a good crowd.

After lunch Jack called. "I've got a piece of what I'm looking for," he said. "There may be more to come. It turns out after the suicide the Oakwood Police got in touch with Smith and Wesson and asked for information on the gun. Smith and Wesson knew it was part of the lot that had gone to NYPD and Oakwood found out about how it got lost back in '69. They stopped their investigation after that."

"Any reason?"

"I got a roundabout explanation that boils down to the fact that Larry Filmore was a good guy who lived in town and he'd died a terrible death and why make more trouble? I didn't exactly hear those words, but I got the feeling that what they weren't saying was that Laura asked them to stop."

"And it's a small town, so they did." It wasn't far-fetched. The police here in town often go out of their way to be nice to residents.

"Right."

"So maybe you'll find out where Larry Filmore got the gun and maybe you won't."

"That's about it. But it'll take some time."

"It's twelve years. How much difference can another few days make?"

In the afternoon I took Eddie to a friend's house, his friend, that is, and came home to read and think. As I walked through the kitchen on my way to the family room, I saw the persimmon. I touched it carefully. It was still un-blemished but softer than when I had brought it home. I took it to the sink, feeling like a kid doing something wrong, peeled back the very thin skin at the top, and took a bite out of the flesh.

It was truly heavenly. I had never tasted anything like it. With half my face wet, I sucked the delicous fruit into my mouth and relished it. I had never tasted anything so good.

I laughed when I had finished it. My face and fingers were wet and I washed them with soap, patting myself dry with a paper towel. Next fall, I would remember to buy a couple for another fall treat.

20

A little while later Jack called to say he had asked a friend in the Firearms Unit of NYPD to look into the history of the Smith & Wesson that killed Filmore. "I told him a little about the Filmore case and I think I got him interested. I didn't want to ask Oakwood to do this because they made a decision twelve years ago to let it be and I don't want to sound like I'm critical. This way, if nothing turns up, Oakwood doesn't know about it."

"Where's he going to look?"

"Probably with the Bureau of Alcohol, Tobacco and Firearms. They have a massive database in Atlanta, Georgia. If the gun passed through a legitimate gun dealer, there'll be a record. If it didn't, we're dead."

"Maybe it was used in the commission of a crime before Filmore killed himself," I said.

"Then it would be in custody somewhere and it wouldn't have killed Filmore."

"Right. Well, let's hope something turns up."

I wasn't very hopeful. Whoever had stolen the gun from Officer Reilly during that snowstorm in 1969 wasn't likely to have walked into a gun dealer and offered it for sale. On the other hand, it might have passed through many hands and ended up with a legitimate dealer after a long sojourn.

I called Joseph after dinner and told her what Laura had

confessed. "It looks as though you were right. It was Laura, not her husband, who was being blackmailed."

"And she's still afraid to come forward. I wonder what the evidence is that concerns her so much. Maybe she tried to bribe the survivor in the other car and he grabbed her handbag or her wallet."

"With her fingerprints on it," I said.

"I'm going to withdraw that. She'd probably just say she was robbed. It must be something else. I'll think about it, Chris. But you've begun to break down her defense. She may tell you more if you give her some time."

"I hope so. Did you get to your meeting on time the other day?"

"I was embarrassingly late," she said with a laugh. "But the participants were discussing something so intensely, they didn't even see me come into the room. And although I know it's not an excuse, I really feel I benefited from that discussion at lunch. I hope you never give up these exercises of yours."

I promised her I would remain open to anything that came my way. I found it interesting that she referred to my investigations as "exercises." Often I felt that way about them myself, but only at the beginning. Somehow, becoming involved in the personalities, the human side of these mysteries, took a toll on me. I now knew something about Laura Filmore that she didn't want me to know, something that was a blot on her life. She had left the scene of an accident in which someone may have been killed, and she may have been responsible. From the way she described it, it sounded as though either car could have caused the accident, and that made me feel that she knew she was at fault and couldn't admit it. I didn't want to tell the police about it, but I rather hoped she would decide to do it herself.

In the evening the phone rang and Jack got up and answered it. He brought it to me from the kitchen. "Someone named Franklin," he said.

"Oh, that's Connecticut." I took the phone. "Hello?"

"Chris? . . . This is Michelle Franklin. You were up here a couple of days ago?"

"Sure. What's up?"

"Well, like you said, sometimes you think of something."

"Yes, tell me." I felt a surge of energy.

"One of the times you were here you mentioned barns and caretakers' cottages? You know, Frannie Gallagher had one behind her house a long time ago."

"How long?"

"I couldn't tell you. But someone lived there once in a while."

"There's nothing there now," I said.

"It burned down."

"Really. Do you know when?"

"I don't remember, but a long time ago. Years."

"Before or after Darby Maxwell was lost in the woods?"

"You've got me. It's just I was talking to my husband and he remembered the fire. The barn was back near the woods and we were afraid there'd be a forest fire. We could see the flames from our house."

"But there wasn't a forest fire," I said.

"No. The firemen came and put it out. But it was a real eyesore for a couple of years. The Gallaghers left it that way for a long time. Every time you drove by you saw the blackened wood. Finally, they got it cleaned up."

"Do you know who stayed there?"

"No idea."

"Man or woman?"

She said, "Mm. I really couldn't tell you."

"Thank you very much, Michelle."

* * *

"Doesn't mean much," Jack said when I told him. "You've seen a lot of secondary structures up there. People don't even remember who they rented to ten or twelve years ago."

"True. But it's something to keep in mind. Maybe I'll call the police up there tomorrow and ask if they have a date for that fire."

"Can't hurt. And meantime, we'll see what BATF comes up with."

I don't know when it struck me that something Laura said didn't ring true. Maybe when I came downstairs on Friday morning to make breakfast.

"The persimmon's gone," Jack said, coming into the kitchen.

"I ate it yesterday. I meant to tell you. Laura was right. It's a heavenly experience. I've never tasted anything like it. And to think she picked them from trees when she was a kid."

"No kidding. She's a southerner?"

"Is that where they grow?"

"Yeah, in the South. What's wrong?"

"She's from Wisconsin."

"She tell you that?"

"Yes. I asked her. It didn't occur to me till you said that."

"Maybe she went to school in Wisconsin."

"Maybe," I said.

"But you're not sure."

"I'm not sure at all."

After Eddie was in nursery school, I called the police in Connecticut and asked about the Gallaghers' barn or cottage. I said I had heard they had one that burned down.

The officer I talked to sounded harried and said he

really didn't have time right now to look into it, that he didn't remember anything about it. He didn't ask for my phone number to get back to me, so I figured he didn't want to. And from the sound of his voice, he may not have been around ten or twelve years ago. I hung up and tried to think where to go from here.

Finally, I called Michelle back. "I'm trying to track down the date of the fire at the Gallaghers'," I said. I told her the response of the police. "Is there some way I can reach the firehouse without going through an operator?"

"Just a minute."

I listened while she flipped pages. "Here's their non-emergency number." She dictated it. "I'm not sure you'll get a fireman if you call now—they're volunteers, you know—but I seem to remember a friend of mine telling me some of the firemen who have jobs in the area drop in there to have lunch together."

"Looks like I'm going back to Connecticut," I said.

"Cheer up. They're nice guys. Bring along a sandwich and you can have lunch with them."

It sounded like a good idea. I put together my old standby, tuna on whole wheat, grabbed a bottle of juice and a napkin, and took off. I had been to only one other firehouse to talk to the volunteers, and that was a couple of summers ago when we were out on Fire Island and the fire chief was murdered. I remember that the men were very helpful and had a lot of records that proved quite useful.

I found the firehouse by following Michelle's directions. A few cars were parked outside, and I left mine next to them and went inside. Shiny fire trucks took up half the space. In the other half, several men were sitting at a table with brown-bag lunches open in front of them.

"Hi!" one of them called. "Help ya?"

"Michelle Franklin told me you meet here for lunch. I'm up from Oakwood, New York. Can I join you?"

"Sure. Pull up a chair. There's lots of room." Actually, he got up and got the chair for me.

I sat down and opened my lunch. I told them I was interested in when the fire at the Gallaghers' had taken place. The men were all old enough that they would remember it. I had a feeling it was the older ones who met here.

"Gallagher," the man who had invited me in said. "I remember that one. Little house out back. That was some time ago. Can you wait till we're finished eating?"

"Sure."

"What's your interest?"

I told them I was looking into the death of Darby Maxwell.

"We were all on that search party," one of the men said, putting a fat sandwich down on a piece of paper towel. "That was real sad. Poor guy didn't know where he was, didn't have a chance. Had some cold nights while he was in the woods. That's what did him in."

We talked about it for a while. They described how they went through the woods in a long line, following the trackers and sheriff's bloodhounds, how they called Darby with a loudspeaker.

"It was like he wasn't there," one of the men said. "And then suddenly he was there and he was dead."

It was like he wasn't there. I didn't comment on that, but it was what I had come to believe.

When all the sandwiches were eaten and all the beer and soda drunk, we cleaned up after ourselves and a man named Mike took me into the fire chief's office. There were pictures of his family on the desk, three generations of them. Mike went to the big file cabinet in a corner of the room and started looking through it.

"Gotta be ten years ago," he said. "We never found out what caused it. Probably a match or a candle or somebody smoking carelessly."

"Was anyone living there when it happened?"

"Apparently not. Place was empty. Gallaghers were away."

"They were away?"

"Yeah, they take a lot of trips. He works at home, so he makes his own hours. She's at the hospital, I think, but not full-time. Nice life."

I agreed, watching him go through the files. "If it was a match or a cigarette, someone must've been there."

"You'd think so, wouldn't you? Could be someone broke in while the Gallaghers were away. We called them where they were at, but they were coming home the next day anyway. Here it is." He pulled a folder out of the drawer. "Gallagher. Guest cottage. Looks like it happened about twelve years ago."

I felt a chill. "Twelve years? That would make it the year Darby Maxwell died."

"No kidding." He turned pages. "Wanna look?"

"Please." The fire had taken place after Darby's death. The structure that had burned down had a living room, kitchen, one bathroom, and two bedrooms, all on one floor. It was built of wood and furnished. Nothing had been salvaged from the fire.

"Did it ever occur to you that it might be connected to Darby Maxwell's disappearance and death?"

Mike looked at me with a frown. "I don't get what you're driving at."

"One of the men at the lunch table, Pete, I think, said, 'It was like he wasn't there.' Maybe he was in that guest house for a few days before he died."

"You mean like he broke in looking for shelter?"

"I have some ideas, but they're not conclusive. I think someone in that little house may have held Darby hostage, hoping to get his mother to pay a ransom."

"Wasn't any ransom asked for that I ever heard."

"I know. Are you sure the Gallaghers were away?"

"Oh, yeah. The police called them somewhere in Europe, France maybe. The Gallaghers were away when that house burned down."

And it wasn't likely they'd just arrived in France if they were coming back the next day. "Then maybe someone else was using the house."

"You got me. All I did was answer the call."

"Who reported the fire?" I asked.

"The family next-door. Franklin, I think it says. There were some other calls, too."

"There aren't any names?"

"Folks don't always give their names. They pick up a phone, call it in, and go about their business. Nowadays with nine-one-one, we know where the call comes from, even if they don't identify themselves. It's cut way down on false alarm calls."

I gave him back the file folder. "Thanks, Mike."

"You look troubled."

"I am. I'll have to talk to the Gallaghers again."

"What can they tell you? They were three thousand miles away."

That was the problem.

"Frannie's at work," Dave Gallagher said.

"Maybe you can help me."

"Come on in."

We went into his office, a cluttered room with two computers, stacks of books and papers on the floor, a bookcase filled with books arranged both vertically and horizontally, and a window that looked out on the woods. Dave took a seat behind his desk and waved me to the other chair in the room. I unbuttoned my coat but left it on. The house was cool, but he plugged in an electric heater and closed the door.

"Big money saver when you heat just one room," he said with a smile.

"It's nice that you're able to work at home."

"Gives us a lot of leverage. And Frannie can almost make her own hours, too. We like traveling and this makes it easy."

"I know you told me you never have a house sitter when you're away, but I heard you used to have a guest cottage out back."

"That was some time ago. It burned down while we were on a trip."

"Did you rent it out or invite anyone to stay in it?"

"We used it like a guest cottage. We have friends that live far away and it was nice to give them a private place to stay. But when it was gone, we decided not to rebuild it. We never found out what caused the fire and we didn't want to take any more chances."

"I was just over at the firehouse," I said. I didn't want to give the impression that I was checking up on him and his wife, but I didn't know how else to put it. "They told me your guest house burned down when Darby Maxwell was lost in the woods."

"Is that when it happened?"

"Yes."

"I don't see the relevance."

"Did you keep the guest house locked?"

"Sure. We didn't want trespassers."

"Was there a phone in the guest house?"

"Never."

"I thought maybe Darby spent some time in there when he got lost."

"In our little house? How would he get in?"

"Maybe he broke a window," I suggested.

"I suppose that's possible." He didn't look as though he believed it.

"Or maybe someone was there already to let him in."

"How would I know that?" Dave Gallagher said. "This is pure speculation, and if we were in Europe we're not responsible for some tramp breaking into our house."

"That's true. I just wondered if you had given the house to someone while you were away."

"We didn't. We told you. We never had a house sitter."

"When you came back, after the fire, did anything look strange to you? As if maybe someone had been inside?"

He smiled. "There wasn't anything left to look strange. The guest house burned down to the ground. What was left was a bathtub and a sink. Anything combustible went up in smoke."

"I see."

"It was a shock to see it when we came back. It was a real nice little house. But it was made of wood and it burned right down to the concrete slab. The furniture was gone; the dishes were cracked and coated with black soot. It was a mess."

I stood up and buttoned my coat. The room had gotten pleasantly warm as we talked. "Thanks for your time," I said.

He looked troubled. "What makes you think someone was in that guest house?" he asked.

The truth was that I couldn't think of any other place Darby could have been together with Larry Filmore, but that wasn't the kind of answer I could give him. "It seemed logical," I said.

"That doesn't mean it happened."

"No. I guess it doesn't."

21

I drove home thinking about what Dave Gallagher had said. It was certainly true that logic didn't have to equate with reality. Yet the coincidence of the Gallaghers being away and the guest house burning down during that period of time seemed too great to attribute to chance. My theory was that after whoever had been blackmailing Larry Filmore had seen to it that Filmore died, he then let Darby go in the woods, as far away from the Gallaghers' as he could manage, and then went back, set fire to the guest house, and went on his way. Perhaps he was one of the anonymous callers reporting the blaze, perhaps not. Michelle Franklin might not have seen the fire or smoke for some time, as the guest house had been on the far side of the Gallaghers' house, the right-hand side, and not visible from the Franklins'. There had been a sketch in the file at the firehouse that had shown that quite clearly.

I had no doubts about the Gallaghers themselves. It seemed pretty clear that they were away at the time of the fire and probably during the whole period that Darby was lost. Was it possible that Filmore's blackmailer just happened to break in, then found Darby, called Larry Filmore, and went on from there? And all of it just happened to take place while the Gallaghers were away? What telephone had the blackmailer used? Twelve years ago half the population didn't walk around with a phone in their pocket. The person had to have a car. Hiking into town to use a phone and buy food seemed improbable. It was almost as though someone who knew the Gallaghers knew they would be away and decided to use the guest house. And that would mean the Gallaghers should have a good idea of who the person was.

By the time I got home I had convinced myself that Dave Gallagher had not told me the whole truth. With the guest house long gone, there were no remains to sift through. I could never find out if the door of the guest house had been opened with a key or broken into. Windows often burst during a fire, so broken glass would not signify a break-in to the firemen examining the ruins. Perhaps the intruder, if that is what he was, had simply lit a match, set some upholstery or a rug on fire, and left the building, waiting to be sure there was a good fire before driving away.

I picked up Eddie and we went home, the conversation far from what had occupied my mind in the preceding hour. He had talked to his nursery school class, and almost everyone was coming to the birthday party. He was very excited. And Elsie was baking a special cake.

"That'll be a great cake," I said.

"I like Elsie's cakes."

"I know you do. You've been eating them since you were just a baby."

"I want ice cream at the party, too."

"That's on my list. Daddy and I thought it would be fun to have pizza."

His face lit up. "A big pizza?"

"Yes. There'll be plenty for everybody."

"That's gonna be a good party."

"You bet."

There was a message from Jack on the answering machine, but it was too late to call him back. He would be on his way home. I hoped it meant he had heard back from his friend who was trying to trace the gun. When he got home in time for dinner, he said he had a bunch of things to tell me.

I could hardly wait, but as usual we did wait. Eddie had to tell Jack about the party, and there was a bath and reading before he went to sleep. Finally, Jack and I sat down to talk.

"I think the gun that killed Larry Filmore had a long uncharted history," Jack began. "After it was stolen from Officer Reilly in 1969, it got from New York down to Florida, but it took about ten years. In 1979 it turned up in a pawnshop/gun shop in Boca Raton. The person who bought it was a young guy named Paul Norman, twenty-five years old, clean record, getting a job as a security guard. He needed to provide his own gun for the job. And that's the last we know about the gun till it turned up in Larry Filmore's garage."

"That's kind of disappointing," I said. "I had imagined it belonged to some lowlife who would blackmail the Filmores."

"It did. Paul Norman has a sheet you wouldn't believe. He started out as a security guard with his own gun and a clean record, but he started getting into trouble a couple of years later—drugs, gambling, you name it."

"He has an arrest record?"

"You bet."

"Then they must have confiscated the gun."

"He never had it on him when he was arrested, and he claimed to have lost it. I got an inch of paper faxed to me this afternoon." He took it out of his briefcase and showed it to me. "It's all here. The last time he was arrested was about four years ago. He's doing a bit in the Florida Correctional System. Right now he's a guest at the North Broward Detention Center."

"I wonder if he's our man," I said. "He could have sold the gun to someone years ago."

"Always possible. But from the sheet, he looks like the kind of guy you're after."

I took the papers from Jack and started looking through them. The photos of Paul Norman, front and side, showed a sullen-looking young man at his first arrest. In subsequent pictures, he got older and angrier, his hair sometimes short, sometimes long, his face sometimes clean-shaven, sometimes bearded, sometimes just not shaven. At his best he wasn't very pleasant-looking.

I knew I could show Laura the pictures and ask her to identify the man, but I wasn't sure that was the way to go. She didn't want to be linked to the accident she had run away from, and she had asked me to stop my investigation.

"What are you thinking?" Jack asked.

"What my next move is."

"You can talk to Paul Norman."

"Why would he admit to another felony? Another couple of felonies, especially homicides? He may have caused Larry Filmore's death and Darby Maxwell's death, he may have blackmailed the Filmores, but none of that is part of his record."

"What is it you want?" Jack asked.

"I want to know who's responsible for the deaths of Darby Maxwell and Larry Filmore."

"You want to tie someone to the Filmore blackmail?"

"I feel very conflicted about that, Jack. I don't want to cause Laura any more trouble."

"I'm not sure you have a choice. The death of Laura's husband seems to be connected to that old accident. You prove one connection, you'll probably have proven the other. I have an idea, but I don't know if you'll like it."

I didn't ask what it was till I had thought about it. Everything was very tenuous. All I had was a series of incidents that had happened at the same time. The only hard evidence was two pairs of men's sneakers that had been identified as belonging to Larry Filmore and Darby Maxwell. There was really no case if I didn't come up with another crucial piece of hard evidence or an admission by the Gallaghers that Paul Norman had spent two weeks in their guest house twelve years ago. "Tell me your idea," I said.

"We get the Florida system to offer Norman a deal like time served for his current felony if he turns over the evidence he said he had in the accident Laura was involved in."

"Then she's in big trouble."

"It happened a long time ago—we don't know how long because she won't say—and I think it's very likely she can get a reduced sentence like community service, especially since this guy blackmailed her."

I felt like I was going in circles. "But if Paul Norman did all these terrible things, I don't think he should go free."

"He won't. As soon as he agrees to the deal, we'll rearrest him for blackmail and see if we can tie him to Filmore's death. And Darby's."

"That's really deceitful," I said.

"You think it's immoral to play a trick on someone who took two innocent lives?"

I did, actually, although I wanted very much to find the person responsible for Darby's death. I knew Jack didn't need my permission to set in motion a deal with Paul Norman. He had all the facts I had, and he knew the procedure. I just wasn't sure I wanted him to do it. "Let me sleep on it. OK?"

"Fine with me."

I thought about it for half an hour, weighing possibilities, trying to come up with alternatives. Finally, I went to the phone and called the Gallaghers' number. If Dave answered, I would hang up. I wanted to talk to Frannie, and I wanted to hit her with a question she wasn't expecting. The kind of work she did was probably done only during the day, so there was a good chance she would be at home at night. I listened to the rings.

"Hello?" It was Frannie.

"Mrs. Gallagher," I said, not introducing myself, "I have some news about Paul Norman."

"Paul? Has something happened? Is he all right?"

Pay dirt, I thought. "This is Chris Bennett," I said. "I think we need to talk."

"Oh." She sounded let down. "I can't."

"It's very important."

"Not over the phone."

"Tomorrow morning then."

"All right. Don't come before eleven." She hung up.

I left after leaving the makings of lunch for Jack and Eddie. I had given Jack permission to try to get Paul Norman to turn over whatever evidence he might have in the accident involving Laura in return for some kind of deal. I didn't like it, but I was now certain he was my man.

I got to the Gallaghers' house a few minutes before eleven. It had snowed overnight in Connecticut, and I could see that a car had backed out of the garage and not come back. I drew up in the fresh snow beside the tracks. When I got inside, I saw that Frannie was alone.

"Kitchen OK?" she asked.

"It's fine."

"How did you know?"

"It's a long story. What's more important is your relationship with Paul Norman."

"That's a long story, too. He's my cousin, my cousin's son. He lived for a while in my parents' house. His mother had a tough life and she couldn't always take care of him and hold a job, so he stayed with us for a couple of years. I can't tell you how much I loved him." She seemed near tears.

"I'm sorry," I said.

"He was like a little brother to me. He was a good boy; he really was. He didn't get in trouble till he was in his twenties."

"Where was this, Frannie?"

"I grew up in Florida. My mother still lives there. My cousin, Paul's mother, died a few years ago. Everything that could go wrong for her did. And for him, too."

"Do you know where he is now?" I asked.

"He's in prison. I thought you knew that."

"I just wondered if you did. I want to know about Paul and the guest house."

She sighed. "He called me once and said he was in New York and could he visit. I said, 'Sure; come up. We have a guest house you can stay in.' "

"When was this?"

"I don't know. Years and years ago. Maybe twenty years, I'm not sure. He was in New York when he called. He drove up and stayed a week or so. Then he left. Then he got in trouble. One day he called again and he came up and stayed for a few days again. Dave never liked him, but he was family. I couldn't turn him down."

"Did he have a key to the guest house?"

"I suppose he could have had one made. He always gave me back mine before he left."

"So he could have come anytime he wanted," I said.

"He always called first. He respected me. He wouldn't just come out of the blue."

"Tell me about twelve years ago."

"When the boy died in the woods."

"Yes."

"I don't know what I can tell you. We weren't here."

"But Paul was."

She looked at me with full eyes. "I don't know that for sure. All I know is we got a call from him in August from Florida and he said he was thinking of coming up north and could he use the guest house. I told him we would be away, but he could stay if he wanted to. I left the key under the mat."

"Did you talk to him when you came back and found the guest house burned down? Did you ask him how it happened?"

"I never knew where to call him," she said, looking as though this was all too much for her. "I didn't know if he'd been here."

"But you knew he'd asked."

"Yes. And I knew nothing about the boy who died. I didn't hear about that till later, and I swear to God I never made a connection till you talked to Dave yesterday."

I had no reason to doubt what she had said. If something happened while a person was away, he might not hear about it for a long time, if ever. "I want you to tell me about the automobile accident," I said.

She looked startled. "How do you know about that?" she said, and I knew the whole truth was going to come out.

"Please tell me, Frannie."

"Does it have something to do with the boy who died?"

"I think it may."

"My God." She pressed her lips together and shook her head slowly. "I saw the car the next morning. It was—"

"When was this, Frannie?" I asked, interrupting.

"The accident? I don't know. It was before the guest house burned down, because Paul never came back after that."

"But you don't recall how many years ago it was?"

She shook her head. "Years. I couldn't put my finger on it."

"Go on. I'm sorry I interrupted. You were telling me how you saw the car the next morning."

"The car, yes. It was an old car, but it was in pretty good shape and Paul took good care of it. He was staying with us and he'd gone out the night before. I went outside to pick some vegetables from the garden and I saw the car. The side was all bashed in. I knocked on the guest house door and went inside. He was still in the bedroom, but he came out in a pair of jeans and no shirt. I said, 'Paul, what happened to the car?' He said some bitch had hit it while he was driving home from New York. He said it was a hit-and-run and a friend of his sitting next to him got hurt pretty bad. I asked him if he wrote down her license plate number and he said he had it, but he didn't want to get involved with the police. It was a big car and it was from New York, not Connecticut. Oh, and there was something else. He said he had something of hers, the woman who was driving, and it would prove she was at fault."

"Did he show it to you or tell you what it was?"

"No. But he seemed pretty pleased with himself. Anyway, he said he was able to drive his car to the nearest hospital and he left his friend there."

"What happened to the friend?"

"I don't know. Paul left a couple of days later."

And there was no phone in the guest house and Paul had given no number to anyone. "Did he ever talk about that accident when you saw him again?"

"I asked once about the man who was hurt and he said not to worry. Paul didn't always tell the truth, you know. He lived a strange life."

"Tell me about it."

She sighed again. Recalling these incidents was taking a toll on her. "He was such a cute little boy," she began. "His mother really loved him, but she just couldn't handle taking care of him and earning a living. There was never any father, and that wasn't so common that many years ago. He was a good boy when he lived with us, and he did OK in school. He wasn't the greatest student, but the teachers liked him. He was good in sports; I remember that. He had a few jobs after high school, but when he was in his twenties he got a really good job in security with some company down there. He stayed for a few years and he had a girlfriend and everything seemed to be going well for him."

"And then?"

"I guess things looked better than they really were. He got involved with drugs and all the wrong people. And then he was accused of stealing."

"While he was working in security?"

"Uh-huh. That was the end of the job. It was the end of his life as a normal person."

"Did he go to prison?" I asked.

"Not the first time. But later he did. He just couldn't seem to keep out of trouble. He lost the girlfriend, too. We all hoped she would steer him the right way, but she couldn't. I know she tried. I always thought when he came up here I could influence him, but he kept getting into trouble and nothing seemed to help." She had been looking down at the table or out the window as she spoke. Now she turned and looked at me. "How could Paul have possibly been involved with that young man who died?"

I told her briefly, not mentioning Larry Filmore.

"You think he used that boy to get the mother to pay for his return?"

"I think it's possible."

"I hate to say it, but it sounds like Paul. It's the kind of thing he would do. Trouble just seemed to fall into his lap and he would take advantage of it. You don't think he actually killed that boy, do you?"

"Not directly. I think he may have taken him into the

woods and pointed him in a wrong direction to get him lost. The young man died of exposure. There were some cold nights during the time he was lost."

"Oh, Paul," she said, putting her head in her hands.

"I'm sorry to have brought up all these painful memories."

"It's not your fault. I wish his life had been different. I wish he had made his life different."

"Thanks, Frannie. I think I have all the facts I need now."

"I don't see what the accident has to do with anything."

"There's a little more that I didn't go in to. I think he kept that to himself."

"He said the woman in the other car was at fault," she said plaintively.

"She may have been."

"I hope so. He's got enough on his plate as it is."

22

"Well, you've tied him to the right place in Connecticut at the right time," Jack said after I got back and told him about my conversation with Frannie Gallagher, including the fact that Paul Norman claimed to have evidence in the accident.

"What about you? Make any progress?"

"I got a callback from Paul Norman's lawyer. He doesn't know anything about an accident or evidence, but he'll talk to Norman as soon as he can and get back to me."

"You probably won't hear till Monday. I'm surprised you even got him on a weekend."

"He sounds like a go-getter, young, activist. He may try to talk to Norman today."

"How did you put it to the lawyer?"

"I said we were looking for the driver of the second vehicle in an accident that happened twelve or more years ago that Norman was involved in. I didn't say a word about Darby Maxwell or Larry Filmore or blackmail or suicide. I gave him a bunch of bullshit, if you want to know the truth, about looking over cold cases and wanting to tie this one up. I had to be careful because I don't know the year or what happened to the passenger who was hurt. I just suggested there could be a recommendation for leniency if we could find the driver of the other car."

"Let's hope we hear."

We didn't hear that day. On Sunday, we picked up Gene and took him to mass and then we all went out for dinner. When we brought Gene back to Greenwillow, Virginia McAlpine was there and she asked me what had happened to my inquiry about Darby Maxwell.

"It was quite some time ago that we spoke," she said. "Has anything happened?"

"A lot has happened," I told her. I said I had visited Betty Linton and was still looking into Darby's death.

"I'll be interested to hear what you find. I remember how well you did back when the Talley twins were here."

I was struck by how much had happened in the years since that first investigation of mine into a murder that had happened on Good Friday in 1950. I had met Jack and married him; we had had a child who was now almost four. And I had worked on a number of homicides that the professionals had either given up on or failed at. My life was very different from that of the young woman who had been released from her vows only a couple of weeks before learning of the Talley murder.

Shortly after we got home, I got a call from Frannie Gallagher.

"Chris," she said, "my cousin Paul called a little while ago. His lawyer came to see him about that accident we talked about."

"Has your cousin decided to cooperate?"

"Yes. But he wants me to fly down and be with him when he talks to the authorities."

"That's probably a good idea. You're very close to him and you really care about him."

"And I want him to get everything off his chest and see if he can make a clean start."

I wasn't sure there would be a clean start for Paul Norman now or ever, but I didn't say that. "When are you going?"

"I want to go tomorrow. Will you come with me?"

"Oh, my. I don't know." All I could think of was that it would be a burden on Jack and I would have to get Elsie to take care of Eddie while I was away.

"Please," Frannie said. "I don't like the idea of going to a prison. I'm really very nervous about the whole thing."

"I'll call you back," I said.

"What's up?" Jack asked.

I told him. He took out his little book and checked the week ahead. I had done this once before when Eddie was younger and I had to go to Ohio to clear Sister Joseph of a ridiculous charge that could have ruined her life.

"Give it a try," Jack said. "I'm clear this week."

So that's how I happened to go to Florida for the first time in my life. Frannie thanked me profusely and Elsie said it was no trouble at all, just be home in time for the birthday party, which I fully intended.

The next morning, I met Frannie at LaGuardia Airport and we boarded a plane for West Palm Beach.

Frannie and I shared a room in a Holiday Inn, eating a good dinner when we got there. Jack had heard back from Paul's lawyer, Jim Peabody, that his client was ready to talk about the automobile accident. When we got to the hotel, I called the lawyer and arranged for a meeting at nine the next morning.

The lawyer picked us up after breakfast and drove us to Pompano Beach, where the prison was. Frannie was a nervous wreck, clutching my hand as we went inside past security. Jim Peabody was a skinny young man who said he had recently begun to represent Paul Norman, the last of a long line of attorneys who had apparently failed to get his sentence reduced. I hoped young Mr. Peabody had some better-paying clients than this one, or at least clients with better cases.

He seemed familiar with the prison, which indicated to me that he may not have had the kind of clients I thought he needed. He led us to the room where Paul Norman was waiting.

"May I see him first?" Frannie said. "Alone? Just to tell him I'm with him all the way?"

"Go on," I said. "I'll wait out here."

She was inside about five minutes when I was summoned. Frannie's eyes were red and teary. Across from her at the table was a man of forty or so, dark hair thinning, clean-shaven, dark eyes looking at me intensely as I came in and took a seat beside his cousin.

"I'm Chris Bennett," I said. I didn't offer my hand.

There were two other people in the room besides the four of us. I assumed at least one of them represented the Florida judicial system. Frannie introduced me to Paul Norman. He said, "Hi," and I nodded, trying to smile.

"Frannie told you about the accident," he said.

"Yes, she did."

"I know who did it."

"Did you ever report it to the police?" I asked.

"I had a friend in the car and he was in bad shape. I had to get him to a hospital. He died there a couple of hours later. A cop came by and I told him what I knew."

This was not a man who told the truth, I thought, unless it was in his best interests. "What can you tell us about the other person involved?"

"She was a good-looking woman, blond, in her forties maybe, diamond ring on her left hand. She hit my car and she ran like hell."

"Did she get out of the car and talk to you?"

"She got out, she saw Barney in the front seat, and she kinda froze. She went back to her car and drove away."

"Is that it?"

"No, that's not it," he said irritably. "She threw something out of the car with her fingerprints all over it."

"What was it?"

"I got it put away. My girlfriend's coming over in a little while. She's got it with her."

"We'll have the prints read and classified," Jim Peabody said. "We'll see if we can put a name to them."

"How're you gonna do that? If she's a housewife somewhere, you won't have her prints on record."

"We have an idea who she is," I said, noting he had been careful not to give up the name himself, saving that piece of information in case we didn't have it ourselves. I didn't want to ask anything that would make Paul Norman admit to blackmailing the Filmores.

"You know this woman?" Paul asked.

"I'm not sure. But I'll do whatever I can to identify her."

His eyes became slits as he looked across the table at me. I wouldn't want to run into this man in the proverbial dark alley.

"Who is she?" Frannie asked.

"We'll find out," I said. "When is your friend coming with the evidence?"

"She should be here now."

"I'll go get her," the lawyer said.

I got up and went with him, leaving Frannie to say a tearful good-bye to her cousin. We retraced our steps through a long hall to the place where we had passed security. A woman was waiting on the other side of the locked gate. She was blond and a little older than I, wearing a raincoat and carrying a large handbag.

"Ms. Wilson?" Jim Peabody said.

She looked at us. "Mr. Peabody?"

"Glad to meet you, ma'am." He offered his hand. "This is Ms. Bennett. She's just been talking to Paul. You have something for us?"

She opened the bag and took out a cigar box with a couple of rubber bands around it. "This is it."

Peabody took it and opened the box, putting the rubber bands around his thin wrist.

"Be careful," the Wilson woman said. "It's old and fragile."

Inside on a nest of cotton was a small plastic bag with a half-smoked cigarette inside.

"A cigarette?" I said in surprise. "What kind of evidence is that?"

"It's marijuana," the woman said, looking at me as though I was completely out of it, which I was. "She was smoking grass while she was driving. She was high. Paul said she swerved into his lane and smacked his car. It was all he could do to keep from going into the other lane and hitting another car. That would've killed him, too."

So that was Laura's secret. She had been smoking marijuana. No wonder she was afraid of being caught, especially if Paul Norman was sober. Jim Peabody closed the box carefully without disturbing its contents.

"We'll turn this over to the police and give you a receipt for it," he said. "Thank you very much for giving it to us."

"Will it get Paul out of jail?"

"I hope so. I can't make any promises, but I'll do my best." He seemed pleased, as though he had finally achieved a long-sought goal.

"Can I see Paul?" Miss Wilson asked.

"I don't think so. It's not visiting hours. We had to set this meeting up special."

"I guess I'll go then." She buttoned her raincoat and hefted the black bag over her shoulder.

"Thank you," I said.

She gave me a little smile and left us.

"What happens now?" I asked.

"I turn this over to the police. They'll take it from there.

You said inside you might be able to help identify this woman in the other car."

"I think I know her. I have something with her fingerprints on it. My husband is a detective sergeant in NYPD and—"

"I talked to him. I know."

"I'll give him what I have."

"Then we should be able to make a match pretty quick—if there's a match to be made."

"Then Mrs. Gallagher and I can go home now?"

"Sure thing. I'll get you to the airport."

"That would be great."

Peabody gave the cigar box to one of the men who had sat in on my interview. Frannie came out a minute later, and the three of us went out to Peabody's car. We had already put our luggage, such as it was, in his trunk so we wouldn't have to go back to the hotel.

After lunch, we flew home.

"It worked out fine," I told Jack that evening. He had picked up Eddie at Elsie's and we had gone out for dinner in the middle of the week, a rare occurrence. "I don't think Paul Norman has any idea that I knew about the car accident before I met his cousin Frannie. It was very convenient that she told me about it. I never mentioned the Filmores and she's probably forgotten their names; at least, she didn't bring it up."

"Very good. I know it bothers you that he's digging himself in deeper, but it doesn't bother me. He's a killer and this may help us get him."

I told him with some embarrassment about my reaction when I saw my first marijuana cigarette. He gave me a smile and a kiss.

"Guess we won't assign you to narcotics."

"That's a relief. But this is a terrible thing that Laura was involved in, if it turns out her prints are on that cigarette."

"I know she's a fine woman, Chris, and I'm willing to bet she never smoked and drove again, but a man died and she should have owned up to it."

"She's paid such a heavy price," I said.

"We'll have to get her prints. It may take a court order."

"I have something with her prints on it," I said. "I'm sure you'll need her later, but this will give you an idea if there's a match." I got up and went to the kitchen where I had left the envelope of snapshots from the birthday party. "She went through the whole pack," I said, handing the envelope to Jack. "And she spent a lot of time looking at the picture of Larry being told he had a phone call. There should be thumbprints on the front and other prints on the back."

"That's terrific," he said. "I guess yours are on the pictures, too."

"Yes, but not on anything you smoke."

"Let's keep it that way." He put the pictures in his briefcase and we talked about other things.

When I got home from teaching the next day, Jack called to say they had lifted some beautiful prints off the snapshots. The best came from the picture I had mentioned. Laura had looked at that one long and hard, realizing so many years later that a problem had arisen during the party and her husband had kept quiet about it.

I took Eddie shopping for some winter shirts in the afternoon. In the morning he had gone to nursery school and I had had my class and we hadn't seen much of each other for the last two days, so we had a good time. Eddie got three shirts, each in a different color, and he carried the bag to the car. Tomorrow was his birthday, and he decided to wear the navy blue shirt for the party.

When Jack came home, he said he had sent off the prints from the photographs and might have a match—or proof that there was no match—by tomorrow, if we were lucky. I wasn't particularly anxious to find out the results. Laura wasn't going anywhere and I had a birthday party to fill my day.

23

On Thursday morning Jack gave Eddie a "teaser" present, as he called it, a softball and a bat. The rest would come later, when Jack came home. Eddie was very excited and wanted to go right outside and start playing, but we explained that Daddy really had to go to work.

"I hope you'll save me a piece of birthday cake," Jack said, putting his coat on.

"A great big piece," Eddie promised. "This big." He held his hands about a foot and a half apart.

"That should do it. See you later." Jack kissed us both and dashed out the door. He was coming home for the party, taking a few hours of what the Department calls "lost time."

When everything was cleaned up, Eddie and I got the dining room table, which we rarely used, ready for the party. We spread out the festive paper tablecloth, put matching napkins and plastic forks and knives at each place, then found the cups and set them out, too.

"I'm sitting here," Eddie said, walking to the head of the table.

"That's the right place," I agreed. "That's called the head of the table, and that's where the birthday boy sits."

"Are you sitting at the table, too?"

"No, I think I'll sit with the mothers, if any of them stay. I ordered enough pizza for lots of people."

"Don't throw it away."

"I won't. I'll freeze it if it's left over and we can have it again."

"When are they coming?"

I laughed. "Not for a long time, honey. It's still morning. They're coming at four. We'll go out around three and pick up the pizzas."

"What time is it now?"

I checked my watch. "It's ten o'clock. They won't be here for six hours."

He seemed surprised that he had so long to wait, but there wasn't much to be done about it. I blew up a bunch of balloons and then I called Elsie to check on the progress of the birthday cake.

"It's all baked," she assured me. "I'm going to assemble it soon and decorate it. Tell Eddie it tastes wonderful."

I did as I was told, assuring him that Elsie would bring it over at the right time. We went out and bought candles, which I had forgotten, and then it was time for lunch.

In the afternoon we picked up the pizzas. I got strict instructions on how to reheat them, as it was still a while till the guests were expected.

When we got home, Eddie said he would put on his new navy blue shirt. I asked if he could do it himself, and he said he could.

While he was upstairs, I got out the paper plates and extra napkins. I had gallons of milk and soda in the refrigerator, although I was pretty sure it was the soda everyone would want. While I was getting things done, Elsie arrived with the most beautiful cake in the world.

"Elsie, how did you do it?" I enthused. "The roses are so perfect. And there's enough butter cream there even for Jack."

"It's a pleasure, Kix," she said, using my childhood

nickname. "It makes me feel like an artist. Go upstairs and get the birthday boy ready. I'll put the candles in."

It was a quarter to four and time for him to be downstairs. I went up to see what was keeping him.

"Did you get your shirt on?" I asked as I came into his room.

"Look."

"That looks pretty good." It was a turtleneck and I smoothed the folded-over fabric at the neck, realizing as I did so that he had put it on backward. I decided it didn't make any difference, and he had obviously worked hard to get it on.

"I like this shirt."

"So do I." I tucked in the back where it was sticking out. That's when I noticed his right hand was tightened in a fist. "What do you have there?" I asked, tapping his fist.

"It's mine," he said. "You can't have it."

"I'm just asking what it is."

"It's mine. I got it from Ryan's brother."

"Can I see it?"

"No."

"Why?"

"Because Ryan's brother said it's a secret. And it's magic."

I could feel my heart start to quicken. "Did you get it at Ryan's birthday party?"

"Uh-huh."

"What is it?"

"A piece of candy."

"Can I see it, Eddie?"

He looked at me as though making a judgment. In that moment, he looked very small and I felt very big and overbearing. "You can see it, but it's mine." He opened his fist slowly. In his hand was a little ball of chocolate.

"Can I have it, Eddie? Just to look at?"

"No!" He made a fist again. "It's mine."

"I know it's yours, but I really need to see it."

He opened his fist again, his eyes on mine. I knew I had to take it from him and I knew he would be angry, but sometimes you just have to do what's right, especially when your child's health is concerned. I grabbed for it and Eddie burst into tears. He screamed and kicked, and as I was trying to pacify him I heard the doorbell ring.

I pulled a tissue out of my pocket and wiped his eyes although he hadn't stopped crying. "Let's go downstairs, Eddie. Someone's at the door."

"I want my magic candy."

"We have lots of candy downstairs, lots and lots of candy."

"That's my magic candy. Ryan's brother said—"

The doorbell rang again.

"Come on, honey. Someone's here for the party. Let's go."

We went downstairs, where Elsie had just opened the door for the first guest. In a few minutes, Eddie was himself again, delighted to be given a beautifully wrapped present from a nursery school friend. A minute later, Mel arrived with Sari and Noah and more packages. I slipped into the kitchen and put the chocolate ball in a plastic bag, then hid it on a high shelf. The doorbell kept ringing and friends kept coming. Jack showed up at the back door, but I was too busy to tell him what I had found. Maybe it was the answer we had been looking for.

There is something touching about a party that is over, about the leftover wrappings and balloons and streamers and paper plates with pieces of cake and puddles of melted ice cream on them. The beautiful paper tablecloth was ripped and doused with soda; napkins lay on the floor; balloons wallowed in corners.

My son was four. He had a life of his own, filled with friends who were important to him. He made choices, played games, sang songs, and misbehaved with the best of them. I felt weary and teary as I gathered up the leavings, grateful that Aunt Meg had a table pad made decades ago to protect the wood. Today it had paid for itself.

Eddie was upstairs sleeping, Elsie had gone home, and Jack had taken the magic ball of chocolate to the hospital to have it analyzed. After everyone had gone and I had told Jack about it, he had asked Eddie some questions. Eddie didn't remember Ryan's brother's name, but I recalled that an older brother had been at the party, now well over a month ago. I hadn't said anything to Pat Damon, Ryan's mother, because I didn't want to agitate her before we knew if there was anything besides chocolate in the ball.

Eddie had said that the brother had given the magic balls to some of the children at the party and told them not to eat them till they were home. He said they would give the kids good dreams. I wondered if he had eaten one himself. Eddie had been given one and had found a second one on the grass. Somehow it had turned up this afternoon and he decided to eat it before his party. I had appeared at his door at a most auspicious moment.

I filled a large plastic bag with what was now garbage and took it out to our garbage can. It would be collected tomorrow. I went back to the dining room to see what damage had been done. I didn't want to run the vacuum while Eddie was sleeping, so I had some work for tomorrow morning. I put the table pad away and replaced the centerpiece. Except for the occasional balloon bouncing as I passed, the dining room looked pretty civil again.

Jack had mentioned that there was no news on the fingerprints and I was rather glad. One thing at a time, I thought. I was happy to have a large chunk of cake in the refrigerator and a ton of pizza slices in the freezer and re-frigerator. I wasn't sure I would suggest pizza again as a quick meal for a long time.

My work done, I sat down in the family room with the paper, which I had barely looked at this morning. By the time Jack got back, I was fast asleep.

Friday was a pretty normal day. On Saturday Elsie and Gene were coming over to help celebrate Eddie's birthday without the crowd. There was plenty of pizza, a favorite of Gene's as well as ours, and I would get some fresh cup-cakes for the occasion. I wasn't sure how we would all tol-erate so much sweet stuff, but I knew we would try. In between, Eddie had nursery school this morning, which left me alone to put the house in order. As soon as he was gone, I went up to his room and checked every drawer to see if any more of the little candy balls had been secreted. I didn't look forward to telling Pat Damon the source of the illness that had marred her son's birthday, if it turned out that the candy balls contained some poison, but I wanted to know as soon as possible if that was it. Jack had turned over the plastic bag to the same emergency room doctor whom we had seen the night of Ryan's party, and he had promised to send it along to whoever would analyze it.

I found nothing in Eddie's drawers except the clothes that were supposed to be there, and I was relieved. I won-dered for a moment which child had been spared a night of agony by accidentally losing his magic candy ball. And I was very thankful that Eddie had put his second one away and not eaten it.

He came home from nursery school and we had lunch together. He asked for pizza, but I said we would have pizza and a salad tonight. For lunch we would stick to what I considered healthy food, an egg salad sandwich and some carrot sticks. He was tired enough after lunch that he took a nap. I sat down with the paper and a moment later the phone rang.

"Got word on the prints," Jack said as I picked up.

I held my breath for a moment, then said, "Tell me."

"They're hers, no doubt about it."

I hadn't expected anything else, but I felt a wave of sadness. "What are you going to do?"

"I'm not taking it to the Oakwood Police yet. I have a feeling—"

"About what?" I asked, surprised at his hesitation.

"You know, when Larry Filmore died, the police did a quick check of his background."

"And found nothing."

"Right. Did anyone check Laura's background?"

"Why should they?" I heard myself sounding annoyed. "She didn't kill him, Jack. We know who killed him. It's just a matter of proving it or getting him to admit it."

"I don't dispute that. I'm just feeling a little itchy about Laura. She was at least partly responsible for a man's death and she evaded the law. I want to see if there's anything else."

"There isn't," I said firmly.

"You may be right," my husband said with a tone of voice I had heard before. "Let me just run her prints through NCIC and see if we come up with anything."

"You won't."

"Boy, would I like a piece of rare roast beef for dinner," he said with mock enthusiasm.

"Roast beef! Roast beef! I have a refrigerator full of pizza."

"Well, I guess that'll have to do."

"And most of the leftover slices have mushrooms and pepperoni."

"I'll force myself."
"You better."
"See you later."

I asked him when he came home if anything else had
turned up. He said no, but he'd left our number in case
something did. This wasn't exactly a priority request, so it
might not be processed for some time. All over the
country, police departments were researching the back-
grounds of people arrested for crimes they had just committed and attempting to match prints found at the scene of
some crime committed in the recent past. We had learned
what we needed to about Laura, and Jack had decided to
turn over his evidence to the Oakwood Police after our
little party on Saturday afternoon.

Laura and I had not spoken for several days, and I hoped
she would not call out of the blue. I made Jack promise
that I could talk to her before he spoke to the police. I
didn't look forward to our meeting, but I couldn't just let
her be arrested with no warning.

I must have been very subdued on Saturday because
Elsie asked if I was all right. I assured her I was. She had
gotten Eddie a set of child's gardening tools so he could
help me in the spring and summer, a gift I knew we would
both appreciate. And in her very kind, grandmotherly way,
she had bought a present for my cousin Gene, one of the
miniature cars he collected. You would have thought it was
his birthday, the way his face lit up.

We took Gene to Greenwillow and then drove home.
Eddie wanted to do some digging with his new shovel, but
it was too cold out. He refused to put the tools in the
garage with the big tools, so we took them up to his room
and I reminded him that they were to be used out-of-doors
only. All I needed now was for him to try digging up the
floor.

There were no messages. Jack's parents were vacationing in Florida, which was why they hadn't come out for the birthday party. When they returned, we would probably do it all over again, but for the moment, the parties were behind us.

"You want to talk to Laura Filmore?" Jack asked.

"I thought maybe I'd wait till you hear from NCIC."

He gave me a smile. "You worried she has a record?"

"No, but it doesn't hurt to wait."

"And you don't want to do this anyway."

"Not really. What do you think they'll do to her, Jack?"

"Hard to say. There are a lot of violations involved. She left the scene of an accident and a man died. Not to mention the drug charge."

"This is the wrong way for this to end."

At that moment, the phone rang.

24

It was for Jack and I knew it was about Laura. He spoke in a low voice, listening a lot, asking a few questions, eventually writing notes on a pad near the telephone. I heard a soft whistle, a number of words of surprise, and my heart froze. He was on much longer than I anticipated, and I wasn't looking forward to what he had to tell me when he got off.

Finally, he hung up and joined me in the family room. "You ready for a long story?" he asked.

"Probably not."

"Well brace yourself."

"This is about Laura's prints?"

"That's the beginning," he said.

"Let me hear it."

"Remember the persimmon?"

My head swam a little. "She gave me one. I left it on the counter to ripen. It was delicious."

"Remember what she told you? That they picked them from trees when she was a kid?"

It came back to me. "And she said before that that she grew up in Wisconsin."

"Well, she didn't grow up in Wisconsin; she went to school there. But she may have picked persimmons as a child. She was born in Georgia and her name was Luann Carter."

"Luann?"

"Right. The prints on the picture and the cigarette both belong to Luann Carter, who dropped out of school in Wisconsin, hooked up with a group of radical antiwar young people, and went on a rampage across the country that included stealing cars and money and even left a couple of homicides in their wake."

"This is impossible, Jack." I could feel everything inside me tightening, including my vocal cords.

"I wish it were."

"You said homicides?"

"I didn't get everything he said—he'll fax the whole report to the office—but somewhere in the Midwest the gang robbed a hardware store and killed the owner and a cop who answered a call from a bystander."

"Oh, no."

"There were five people in the gang, three men and two women. Two of the men were arrested after that robbery. The other three got away. They drove west and were involved in at least two other armed robberies before they dropped out of sight. The man was eventually found dead of a drug overdose in San Francisco. The other woman turned herself in when the FBI was closing in on her a few years ago and she made a sweet deal. Luann Carter disappeared off the face of the earth."

"When did all this happen?" I asked, surprised to hear my voice almost a whisper.

"Late sixties, early seventies."

"She was young."

"She was over eighteen."

"She came to New York," I said, putting it together. "She met Larry Filmore; they fell in love and married. She told him she was Laura something and she became Laura Filmore."

"I'd guess that's the short version."

I felt cold, almost to the point of trembling. "She can't have killed anyone, Jack. She's just not that kind of person."

"Not now she isn't. People change. But she's wanted by the FBI."

"Does your contact have her current name and address?"

"Nobody does except us."

"I have to think about this overnight."

"No problem."

It was one of the worst nights of my life. I had cleaned out my aunt's cartons and learned of two deaths. Two men had died and their sneakers had been switched. Now, a month and a half later, I had inadvertently turned up a person wanted for murder, a fine and decent woman who was as good a member of our community as any I had ever met.

I felt as conflicted about this as I had ever felt. I knew I had no choice. Laura had to be turned in. Jack would give me time, but not indefinitely. I had to see Laura soon and then walk away to let the police do their job. All I had wanted was to find Paul Norman and prove he had killed Larry Filmore and caused the death of Darby Maxwell. I had almost, but not quite, done that. It occurred to me that if Laura hadn't been smoking marijuana that night in the car over twelve years ago, both her husband and Darby would still be alive, as well, perhaps, as the man in the car who had died in the accident. It was a terrible what-if. The consequences of that small action had ranged so far and affected so many people, it was hard to accept.

I got up Sunday morning, happy that I was going to mass with my family. When we left the church, we shook hands with the priest, who asked if I was all right.

"Fine, thank you," I said.

"You look a little pale, Chris. Don't let the cold weather get you down."

I promised I would look after myself. We walked out to the car and Jack drove us home. He was cooking today, and I was thankful for that. But it also took away my one possible excuse not to confront Laura.

We got home and divvied up the *Times*, Jack looking at the sports section first, I at the news of the week. I couldn't concentrate.

"You make a decision?" Jack asked.

"I'll go this afternoon."

"You mind if I alert the Oakwood Police about her?"

"After I leave the house, please. And I don't want them moving in on her till I leave. I have to hear her out. I have to give her a chance to explain herself. It may be the last time she can do that. I'm sure she'll call a lawyer."

"Whatever you say."

We had a light lunch and I waited till one, then told Eddie I had to go out for a while, but he could stay home and help Daddy prepare dinner. Eddie liked that, working with Jack, whether it was cooking or hammering nails.

I drove over to Laura's beautiful house and pulled into her driveway. It occurred to me that every day of her life she walked in and out of the garage where she had found her husband's body twelve years ago. I shuddered at the thought.

I walked around to the front door and pushed the button, hearing the musical chimes echo inside. No one answered. I pushed the bell again, waited a moment, and walked away. I had been given a reprieve.

"You looking for Laura?"

I looked around. A woman walking a dog had stopped at the foot of the driveway.

"Yes. She doesn't seem to be home."

"I think she went to the cemetery."

"Did someone die?"

"No, it's some kind of anniversary. Her husband is buried in the Catholic cemetery just at the edge of town."

"Yes, I know it." My aunt and uncle were buried there, having lived and died in Oakwood. "Thank you."

"Sure."

She went on her way, talking to her dog. I got back in the car and made my way out of the small community of large houses that made up Oakwood's most expensive living area. At the main road, I turned toward the cemetery rather than going home.

I could remember the funerals of my uncle and aunt, a number of years apart but both of them after my mother died. I turned into the entrance and went into the main building. A woman at a desk told me where to find the grave of Lawrence Filmore. It wasn't all that far from my relatives.

I located the section and parked my car at the side of the road behind Laura's empty car. As always, it was quiet and peaceful here, the trees bare except for the occasional evergreen. I walked down a path that would take me to the Filmore plot. By the time I saw Laura, sitting on a stone bench and looking off into the distance, I was almost trembling. As I approached, I noticed once again what a good-looking woman she was. Her blond hair seemed to fall just the way she would want it to. Her coat was camel-colored and a brown scarf peeked over the collar.

I had changed my clothes after we came back from church and I looked much more casual than she, but she always looked well and carefully dressed, her nails lacquered, her cheeks slightly pink, whether from the cold or otherwise, I could not tell. I stepped on some dry leaves that crackled, and she turned toward me.

"Chris?"

"Hi. Your neighbor said you were here."

"You came out here to see me?"

"We have to talk, Laura. I thought this was as good a place as any."

She watched me as I neared the bench, then moved over to give me a place to sit. "This is where Larry is buried," she said. "I'll be buried over there, to the right."

The stone was simple, gray granite with a cross on top, his name and the dates of his birth and death engraved underneath. As I often do, I subtracted one date from the other, realizing the difference was exactly fifty, almost to the day. The happy birthday party. It had marked the end of his life. On the grass in front of the stone was a large bouquet of flowers.

"I know," I said.

She nodded. "It was the persimmon, wasn't it?"

"That was part of it."

"You didn't stop when I asked you."

"I couldn't. There was Darby. Betty wanted to know who was responsible for his death and the two deaths were all wound up together."

"Yes."

"I went to Florida, Laura. The man whose car you hit is in jail down there. I talked to him with his lawyer present. He said the man in his car died later that night."

"I know. He blackmailed me, remember?"

"His girlfriend turned over the evidence you threw out of the window that night."

Her eyes teared. "How could I have been so stupid?" she said.

"You were frightened and you panicked. The Florida authorities tested the marijuana cigarette for prints and they lifted some. They match yours."

"Where did you get mine from?"

"The pictures Celia Yaeger gave me."

"You showed me those pictures to get my prints?"

"I showed you those pictures so you would see your husband receiving a phone call during the party. I had no idea of your involvement. Later, I remembered you had handled them."

"And then what?" she said.

"Then your prints were checked to see if there was any more information about you in police files."

"I see."

"And there was."

"So you know it all."

"I know a lot of it. The full report is being faxed to the New York police. We'll see it tomorrow."

"It's not what it seems to be."

"I'd like to hear it from you, Laura."

She got up and walked to her husband's grave, knelt, and moved the flowers slightly, more to take up time, I thought, than for any aesthetic reason. Then she faced me, looking forlorn.

"It was a bad war," she said, "the one we fought in Vietnam. You wouldn't know. You were just a child at the time. I was a student and a lot of us were angry about the war, but no one would listen to us if we spoke softly. So a group of us decided to do it our way."

"Which was?"

"To do things that wouldn't go unnoticed. To call attention to a bad war."

I had the feeling she was picking her words carefully, perhaps that she had prepared for this moment for many years, hoping it would never come. "And how did you do that?"

"We did things that made a splash but didn't hurt anybody. Once we made a huge bonfire in a field outside a small town. We called the local radio station and said that in Vietnam fires like that killed women and children and destroyed their homes. Then we moved on."

"You committed armed robbery," I reminded her.

"We needed money to live, so we took it. I've spent my life giving it back, Chris. Not just money but my time, my energy, my heart and soul."

"Everyone is grateful for that."

"But it isn't enough, is it?" She bent and picked up a twig several inches long, broke it in half, and dropped it on the grass.

"There were two homicides," I said.

"They weren't intentional and I had no part in them. I never shot a gun; I never carried a gun; I never touched a gun."

"Then I'm sure something can be worked out."

"Unfortunately, in that state being an accessory is as good as shooting a gun."

"I see."

"It was a hardware store. All we wanted was what was in the cash register, just enough to eat and buy gas. It was a busy store—we'd watched it—and we went in when it was empty. The owner opened the register and started to take the bills out. All of a sudden, he had a gun in his hand. I was terrified. Maura started screaming. The man with the gun turned toward us and Roger got a shot off. It was a good shot. The man dropped out of sight behind the counter. Next thing we knew, there was a cop in the doorway shouting at us to drop our weapons. Roger shot twice and the cop fell. We ran out of the store and drove away."

She seemed exhausted by the story. She came back to the bench and sat beside me. "Three shots," she said. "Two men dead."

"It must have been horrible."

"It was."

"Did the gang break up then?" I asked.

For the first time, she hesitated. "Not at that moment," she said finally. "We stayed together till we got to California."

"Doing what?" I needed to know, to hear it from her.

"We did some things."

That was it. I had hoped she would say they had disbanded after the hardware store disaster, that Jack's information was wrong, but she didn't.

"I can't describe the remorse I felt," she said after a moment. "I thought of those two lives lost, an older man who had a big family and the cop. I can still see his face in the doorway, very boyish. He was in his twenties. He wasn't that much older than we were. He was newly married and his wife was pregnant. I see his face sometimes in my dreams."

"Why didn't you stop after that incident?"

"It's hard to explain. We needed each other. We couldn't just break up into five pieces on the spur of the moment. And we still needed money."

I thought about it. "Did you have a relationship with one of the men?"

"Maybe. Maybe that was it for me. I never saw any of them after we got to California. Most of them went to jail. I read about it."

"One died of an overdose."

She was still.

"The night of the accident," I said. "You were smoking."

She shook her head. "I was so stupid. I hadn't smoked grass for years. Larry never knew I had smoked it. He didn't know anything about my life before we met. I was with some friends and one of them handed me a joint. I lit up when I was driving. It had more of an effect on me than I remembered. My car probably wandered into the other lane. Of course I shouldn't have been smoking. Of course I shouldn't have tossed it out the window—I saw him in the rearview mirror, picking it up as I pulled away—but I wasn't thinking straight. None of this would have happened if I hadn't been smoking. Larry died because of it."

"And another man," I said.

"Yes." Her voice was very low.

"What did you tell your husband when you got home that night?"

"Just that there'd been an accident, that I'd panicked, and that I was afraid. Later, when the calls began, I told him I'd been smoking. He protected me because he loved me. But on the night of the party, I didn't know where he went until he didn't come home. Then I began to suspect he'd been called by the blackmailer, who we both thought was out of our lives. But I had no idea where he was. And of course, I didn't know there was someone else involved."

I sat quietly. She had lived two separate lives, and now she was about to start a third. There would be lawyers and appearances in court, stories that were true or partly true or completely false. In the end, perhaps there would be a plea bargain, a balance of her old life against her new one, what she had once been weighed against the person she had become. I hoped she would stay out of prison, but I wasn't sure that could be arranged.

Suddenly she looked at me with a smile. "You see why I refused to give you the names of my friends in Connecticut. I knew they weren't involved and I didn't want to get them involved."

I nodded. It seemed so long ago, I had almost forgotten.

"Did he tell you he blackmailed me?" she asked. "The man in jail in Florida?"

"Not yet. We just got the cigarette from him and his description of what happened that night. He doesn't know we know about the blackmail and the murder of your husband. But we've tied the gun to him."

"Larry must have thought he could somehow get himself out of his clutches if they came to the house. Maybe he said he had money in the fishing box."

"That's where you found the gun?"

"Yes. But I guess the killer got suspicious. I wish I'd gotten up when I heard the bang. I wish—"

"Will you turn yourself in, Laura?"

"To the police?"

"You really have to."

"I'll end up in jail."

I didn't know what to say. Suddenly I heard the sound of running feet and someone shouted, "Police! Don't move."

"Oh, no," Laura said.

Three uniformed members of the Oakwood Police Department appeared, all of them holding weapons.

"It's OK, Chris!" I heard Jack call from the path.

I turned toward him and called back, "Where's Eddie?"

"In the car. He's fine."

The police officers were busy handcuffing Laura and reading her her rights as I walked back to where Jack was.

"Chris!" she called.

I took a few steps in her direction.

"Make him pay for killing Larry."

"I will," I promised.

"I guess I can call my mother now," she said, tears forming in her eyes. "She'll see her grandchildren for the first time, and her great-grandchildren."

I turned away. I didn't want to see her taken to the car.

25

I gave a long statement to the Oakwood Police that afternoon while my husband and son made dinner. Larry Filmore had been murdered in Oakwood and they were very interested in what I had learned about his death and the suspect I had uncovered. They didn't really know anything about Darby Maxwell's death, but they got in touch with the police in Connecticut and arranged for someone to come down the next day and take another statement from me. They called the prison in Florida and began to make arrangements for Paul Norman to be brought to New York State for questioning in the two deaths and in the automobile accident as well. It was a complicated business and I had to keep straightening out the chronology and identifying the players. I gave them chapter and verse on the gun that had killed Filmore, going back to the winter of 1969, when one of the cops talking to me had not yet been born.

It was exhausting and I knew I would think of more details when I got home, but I wanted to give them as much as I could today to spare myself another similar ordeal.

When it was over, I asked about Laura.

"She's been taken to the FBI office in White Plains," one of the cops said. "She asked for a lawyer and I think he was waiting for her when she got there."

"I'd like to bring her some things, a toothbrush and some clothes," I said.

He told me whom to call in White Plains. Then I drove home.

Jack and Eddie were having a good time in the kitchen. Something in the oven smelled very good.

"You look like hell," Jack said.

"This was one tough day."

"Go take it easy. We've got everything under control."

It was what I wanted to hear.

I spent a lot of time that night thinking about something I was sure Laura—or Luann—had not thought about until it was too late, consequences. I thought of pebbles thrown into ponds and the ripples they made. I thought of children touching fire, not understanding what would happen to their skin. And I thought of young people stealing and killing for a cause they considered worthy.

How many of them, I wondered, had done what Laura did, simply become someone else and put the past behind them? And how many others had paid a price? I had been born at a different time and not lived through the turmoil of the sixties and seventies at an age when I could have been drawn into the kind of life Laura had experienced. At what age did a person need to accept responsibility for his actions? At what age did he need to think about the consequences of what he did? Had Laura ever accepted such responsibility or thought about those consequences? After all, at an age when she was a wife and mother, and had been for many years, she had driven while smoking an illegal substance and had left the scene of an accident she may have caused.

And still, as she had said this afternoon, she had spent much of her life making restitution. My questions had no certain answers, and that's probably why they kept me awake so long.

The next day I talked to the Connecticut police in my own living room. The detective who came down was old enough that he remembered Darby well, the search parties, the community gathering together to help. I told him about the Gallaghers and their cousin, Paul Norman. I told him about the trip Frannie and I had made to Florida and what we had turned up. I gave him names and numbers and suggestions. When he left, I called Betty Linton and went over a lot of it again. To say she was shocked at Laura Filmore's part in all of it was an understatement.

Later in the day, Jack called. He had heard from the hospital.

"What hospital?" I asked, alarmed.

"About the chocolate."

"Oh," I said with relief, "that hospital."

"They said there was a substance at the center—I don't have my notes right here—that induced vomiting in the kids who ate it. The police are questioning Ryan's brother to see who gave him the candies."

"He's just a boy," I said. "I hope they won't charge him with anything."

"They just want the source, if they can nail it down. The hospital was very grateful that we turned up the candy."

So was I.

Laura Filmore posted a huge bond, over a million dollars, and was released from prison in her own recognizance. She hired a name-brand lawyer who is putting together a defense for her trial, which is scheduled for next year. The town turned out to support her, and I was with them all the way. Her elderly mother came to visit, renewing their once close relationship. It was the first time they had seen each other in over thirty years. I was glad something really good came out of Laura's problems.

Some time later, I heard from Frannie Gallagher. Paul had been flown to New York, where he was questioned by detectives from Oakwood and Connecticut. Confronted with evidence about the gun, the fire at the Gallaghers', and assorted other things, he made a deal that included a confession to having harbored Darby Maxwell in the guest house for several days and not turning him over to the police. He refused to admit he had had a hand in Darby's death.

He also refused to admit he had shot Larry Filmore. Filmore had driven them to Oakwood, he said, promising Norman money that was locked in a box in the garage. But they had gotten in an argument about who would go for the box and Filmore had taken the gun from him and shot himself, after which Norman fled. That's about as believable as some of my son's fantasies. If Larry Filmore had a gun in his hand and Paul Norman was nearby, who would be the most likely target?

When they talk about tangled webs, I think they probably mean situations like that.

The detective from Oakwood who did the questioning was my old friend Detective Joe Fox. We have had our problems in the past, but I have grown to like him very much and to trust his instincts. He called one day and asked if he could come over to talk to me about the case. I invited him for the evening and got a nice coffee cake to serve when he came.

He arrived with flowers, not for the first time, and we all made ourselves comfortable in the family room. Jack had gotten a really good fire going and Eddie was asleep upstairs. It was already December, and a light coating of snow covered all the lawns on the block.

"You get all the good ones, Mrs. Brooks," Joe said, sipping his coffee. He never calls me Chris.

"This one came out of a carton in the basement, some letters and cards my aunt saved. We had a little water down there from an open window and I decided to go through the papers and see what was worth saving."

"But surely your aunt didn't have knowledge of a homicide."

"She didn't, and I didn't, either. I just wanted to meet the people who had written to my aunt. It was the sneakers that made me realize something was amiss."

"The sneakers, right. That was in your statement. I asked Paul Norman about them. From the look on his face, I could tell he didn't know what I was talking about. You want to tell me about it?"

I went through it for the last time, or so I hoped, Larry Filmore's brilliant move to alert the world that something was amiss.

"So why wasn't the world alerted?"

I spelled it out for him.

"Ah."

"And it was only by chance that the two surviving women mentioned the sneakers to me. If they hadn't, none of this would have happened."

"Misplaced sneakers," the detective said thoughtfully. "I'll keep that in mind next time I'm held hostage."

"I hope there's no next time," I said.

"Thank you, dear lady. So do I."

EPILOGUE

It was winter when an envelope with my name and address typed on the front arrived. The return address was a mysterious FG and a street that looked familiar but didn't quite register. I slit it open and pulled out a couple of sheets of paper obviously copied on a machine. A small note-sized paper fluttered to the floor. I picked it up, smiling at the bright flowers along the top.

The note read:

Dear Chris,

I thought you would want to see this. I got it a couple of weeks ago and didn't know whether I should send it along but decided I should. I hope this answers all your questions.

Love,

Frannie

Frannie Gallagher, I thought. I made myself comfortable and began to read.

Dear Frannie,

Peabody says he'll mail this to you without looking at what it says. I want to come clean, at least to you. I owe you that much. It's always bothered me that I burned down the guest house and didn't tell you. I should of paid you, but I was short on cash and after awhile I just forgot. You know me.

I knew you and Dave were going away that time for a couple of weeks ten or eleven years ago, whenever it was, and I had something doing in New York and when I got it done, I figured I'd rest up in Connecticut. I always like it there. So I drove up and made myself at home. All I wanted was a couple of days to rest up and sleep and maybe walk in the woods.

One night there was this knock on the door. When I looked outside, a guy was standing there. I asked him what he wanted and he said he was lost. He came inside and I got the feeling he was a retard or something. He knew his mother's phone number and asked if I'd call her and I probably would of, but there was no phone. I told him I'd have to go into town and find a phone, but it would have to wait till tomorrow.

I gave him one of those frozen dinners I'd picked up at the store and let him sleep in the little bedroom. His name was Darby, which I thought was a crazy name. I don't remember if he gave me his last name.

Anyways, I was pretty short of cash around that time—I know you've heard that before, so don't laugh—and I thought maybe I could get his mother to pay me a little something to give him back. So the next day I went into town and got a paper to see if there was a story about a missing person.

It was on the front page of the local newspaper, how he walked away from his mother and got lost in the woods. They even had a search party out looking for him. I decided to wait another day before I called. I didn't want to sound anxious. I had locked the guy in the bedroom and told him not to make any noise.

So I went back to town the next day and sure enough, there were flyers on all the poles in town. So I called his mother and asked some questions and whether there was a reward. She kind of waffled, but the bottom line was no. I couldn't believe it.

I was pissed, I can tell you. I had thought maybe ten thousand, but I would've taken a thou. I mean, this was her son, for God's sake. So I called someone I knew who had some money.

You remember that car accident I was in when a friend of mine got hurt real bad? Well, the gal who hit my car was married to a guy with lots of money. You already know what she was smoking that night. So I called this guy and told him I needed to see him and I needed some money or someone would die. I also reminded him I had a little something on his wife that I could take to the police. He said he didn't have time for me; I should call back the next day. I think he was at a party or something. He really ticked me off. And this Darby guy was a pain that night, crying and everything, and I called this woman's husband again and put it to him that he better get his ass up here or the butt his wife was smoking the night of the accident would be in a police station and did he know what she would look like after a few years in Girls Town. And I said there would be a dead body in the morning besides. So he came.

The shit only had a couple hundred dollars on him and he didn't want to deal unless I gave him the evidence and the retard was driving me crazy. Finally, the guy said he had money at home and we drove to this town in New York State. What a house. He must've been worth millions. He drove into his garage and gave me a song and dance about having a lot of money in some box in the garage. I knew he was lying. I knew the minute he got out of that car an alarm would go off and I'd be in jail. I was scared to death, Frannie. I didn't know what to do and he was like trying to get my gun away from me. (I had this old gun.) So I had to, well, anyway, he got shot and I fixed it up to look like he shot himself. You know, like a suicide. Then I got the hell out of there.

I had a hell of a time getting back to Connecticut, I can tell you. I was lucky to catch a ride after I got off the train, but I had him drop me a mile from the house. I took Darby into the woods and pointed him in some direction and told him to keep walking and he'd find his mother. Then I went back and tried to clean up the guest house so you wouldn't know I'd been there with two other people. The place was a mess and I had to get back to Florida and I took the easy way out. I took my stuff out and started a fire. When it was going good, I drove into town and called the fire number.

That's the story, Frannie. I'm sorry about everything. I don't know what happened to that Darby guy. Maybe he found another house; maybe he didn't. I just knew I had to get out of there before he started talking to anyone.

Anyway, I owe you. I always have.
Paul

Even after leaving the cloistered world
of St. Stephen's Convent for suburban
New York State, Christine Bennett still finds
time to celebrate the holy days.

Unfortunately, in the secular world
the holidays seem to end in murder—
and it's up to this ex-nun to discover
who commits these unholy acts.

LEE HARRIS

The Christine Bennett Mysteries

THE GOOD FRIDAY MURDER
The First Christine Bennett Mystery
Ex-nun Christine Bennett has only just begun settling
into her new life in suburban New York State when
she finds herself volunteering to investigate a murder
that happened on Good Friday—forty years ago.

THE YOM KIPPUR MURDER
When Christine Bennett discovers that her friend, a
lonely widower living on Manhattan's West Side, has
been murdered, she is determined to solve the crime.

THE CHRISTENING DAY MURDER
Christine Bennett is looking forward to attending the
christening of her friend's baby—until the skeletal
remains of the victim from a thirty-year-old murder
are found in the church basement.

THE ST. PATRICK'S DAY MURDER

Police officer Scotty McVeigh is one of New York's finest, until he is shot on St. Patrick's Day. Speculating that his murder may be connected with the deaths of other off-duty cops, Christine Bennett begins to pursue a killer.

THE CHRISTMAS NIGHT MURDER

When a priest never arrives at his Christmas night party at St. Stephen's Convent, the worried nuns invite Christine Bennett to investigate. But nothing turns up—until an old scandal involving the priest and a novice resurfaces.

THE THANKSGIVING DAY MURDER

Natalie Gordon vanished a year ago at the Thanksgiving Day Parade, and still the police have no leads. Christine Bennett feels compelled to investigate Natalie's mysterious disappearance—and her equally mysterious past.

THE PASSOVER MURDER

For fifteen years, Iris Grodnick's murder during Passover has remained a troubling mystery. Christine Bennett reluctantly consents to look into it for Iris's family one last time—and soon suspects that some of the relatives are not telling her the whole truth.

THE VALENTINE'S DAY MURDER

Three friends disappear after a Valentine's night walk across frozen Lake Erie—and later two are found dead, with the third suspected of the murders. Christine Bennett is offered the difficult task of finding the third friend and proving his innocence, but when she closes in on the truth, she finds herself skating on very thin ice.

THE NEW YEAR'S EVE MURDER

On December 30th, Susan Stark mysteriously disappears after being dropped off in front of her parents' house. Christine Bennett, armed with only a few phone numbers and a photo, steps into the missing girl's life—and meets a Susan with a secret life that may have lured her to a deadly end.

THE MOTHER'S DAY MURDER

When a young woman claims to be the natural daughter of Sister Joseph, beloved Superior at St. Stephen's, Christine Bennett is appalled. But when the girl is murdered and Sister Joseph is the prime suspect, Chris frantically searches for evidence that can save Sister Joseph, her dearest friend, from a life behind bars.

THE FATHER'S DAY MURDER

At a Father's Day reunion dinner of the Morris Avenue Boys, chums since childhood, one of the men stabs to death the group's most celebrated member, novelist Arthur Wien. As Christine Bennett investigates, forty years' worth of secrets emerge, revealing a web of lies, theft, adultery, and blackmail that rivals the darkest plot of the dead man's novels.

APRIL FOOL

THE PASSOVER MURDER

For his favorite charity, the high school drama club, Willard Platt fakes his own murder as an April fool stunt. But when the real thing happens later that same day, Christine Bennett investigates and finds that behind this suburban family's respectable facade, violent passions are seething.

The Christine Bennett Mysteries
by Lee Harris
Published by Fawcett Books.
Available at bookstores everywhere.